MONTANA
Treasures

A Montana Romance

MONTANA
Treasures

A Montana Romance

VELDA
BROTHERTON

GALWAY

OGHMA CREATIVE MEDIA

www.oghmacreative.com

ISBN: 978-1-63373-181-3

Interior Design by Elizabeth Easter
Editing by Gil Miller

Galway Press
Oghma Creative Media
Bentonville, Arkansas
www.oghmacreative.com

To Casey, with love

You who made all of this possible.
Thank you for all you do.

One

Though she missed Reed, Tressie settled in quickly at Lincolnshire's camp. The work of cooking for the miners was much easier than her life had been before she followed Reed from the lonely soddy and left her sad memories behind. And the baby was safe. He flourished in the open-air atmosphere of the mess tent. Many of the miners who worked for Lincolnshire became fond of the child, and it wasn't unusual for one of them to fetch him from his makeshift cradle on the floor beside Tressie. The baby would often spend mealtimes being passed around at the crude tables. His mother soon learned not to worry about him as she served up the generous meals provided the men for four bits.

Since the laborers had come hoping to stake their own claims only to become disillusioned for one reason or the other, they gladly worked for wages: $6 a day in gold that was equal to $12 in greenbacks, if there had been any such thing in the territory, which there was not. Coins worth twelve and a half cents and referred to as "bits" were in good supply. Saloons priced their mugs of beer at a bit. It was convenient. The "pilgrims" who worked for Lincolnshire were paid in gold. Men with their own claims were taking out up to $150 worth of gold a day. The Lincolnshire mine daily fetched out that much for each and every man who toiled there. It was a bitter lesson well learned that the owner takes the lion's share.

Tressie didn't have to worry about collecting the cost of the meals she served. She had but to cook, serve, and clean up after the meals. Lincolnshire had an accountant who kept track of such things as room and board for the miners. He ran, in essence, a company town. A man could board for $1, take his meals for less than $2, and have the equal of $3 left of his daily pay. Prices were high because of the gold strikes, and no one got rich except those who struck gold on their own claims.

Tressie learned all this before she had been cooking in the mess tent a week. She also learned what hard work it was feeding twenty or thirty men three times a day. What appetites they had! She would no sooner finish all the scrubbing up from breakfast than it was time to cook dinner, and the same again for supper. She soon found shortcuts, such as cooking all the potatoes for a day during the morning, or cooking enough stew or beans for two days in the big iron kettle, then keeping it at the back of the stove with a low fire going all night. At long day's end, she often fell asleep while crooning to Caleb in his crate beside her cot. But it was honest work that didn't ask her to sell her self-respect, and she was glad to get it.

Lincolnshire didn't charge her room and board like he did the miners, and soon she had amassed quite a nest egg of gold, which she kept squirreled away in the deer-hide pouch Reed had fashioned for her on the trail. There was rarely time to ride into town and spend what she was earning. She worked seven days a week, for though the miners laid out on Sunday, they still had to be fed. Many of them, however, were absent from Saturday night until the wee hours of Monday morning, out doing their celebrating in town, dancing at the Golden Sun or gambling at the Busted Mule, or bedding the girls anywhere they could find them.

From the perch on the side of the hill Tressie watched in awe as the town of Virginia City mushroomed. Stone buildings soon outnumbered wooden ones. And what a wide variety of businesses there were: bathrooms attached to shaving and hairdressing saloons, a physician and surgeon's office, a Chinese laundry where the dirty wash water was panned daily for stray gold dust. Though Tressie didn't go into town much, she kept abreast of the news, for the miners were wont to gossip and exchange stories while at the table.

Some even brought in copies of the first newspaper in town, the *Montana Post*. In December, Tressie was awed to learn that an honest-to-goodness theater would present the play *Faint Heart Never Won Fair Lady* and planned many more thereafter. She couldn't go, but Rose did and told her all about it during one of their weekly visits.

On that occasion Tressie's beautiful blond friend alighted from her carriage, holding her full, brightly colored skirts up out of the muck while she strode through the center aisle of the cook tent to where Tressie spent the better part of her days. There she picked up Caleb, who sat propped into the corner of his sleeping crate, and parked herself nearby to chatter.

"I wish you could have been there last night. I never saw such shenanigans in my life. The theater was so full you could scarcely wiggle. And people stomped and cheered and laughed and cried, all at the proper times, of course. Folks were only a little more rowdy than a sophisticated city crowd. And after the play they had this wonderfully funny presentation of songs, and a grand overture by a real orchestra. It was delightful."

Caleb gnawed at Rose's finger and crowed with delight.

Watching him with adoration, Tressie smiled at her friend. "Did everybody go?"

"Goodness, no. Some of my girls managed to get someone to take them. I went with Jarrad, of course. But the whole town couldn't have gotten inside. They say we're nearing a population of ten thousand souls. Can you imagine that, Tressie? Ten thousand folks all in one place out here in this wilderness?"

Tressie could not.

"What flabbergasts me," Rose went on, "is that they seem to be here for the winter. I truly thought we'd close down, but here it is December, colder than the hubs of hell, if you'll excuse my swearing, and business is going full tilt. I don't know about you, but I'm ready for a warmer climate."

Rose shifted Caleb across one knee and jiggled him, laughing at the expression on his round little face. Abruptly, she said, "I may just travel back to St. Louis till spring."

The idea distressed Tressie. Rose was the only person she felt a true kinship to, and the thought of going without her Sunday afternoon visits for several months was not a happy one. With the sides of the mess tent now staked down against the brutal cold and wind, she felt like a prisoner enclosed in a dark and very lonely cave. She could no longer gaze out at the mountains while she worked, nor catch a whiff of pine-scented air.

The bubbling pot caught her attention, and she stirred it with a wooden spoon. Rose was right, the weather here had little to offer. Living under such primitive conditions was made all the more difficult in subzero weather. Despite her disappointment, she couldn't blame her friend for seeking the more genteel offerings in St. Louis.

"I'll miss you," Tressie murmured without glancing at Rose. Her own desires, she knew, were written on her face for all to see. A home and hearth, a bed for Caleb, and a man to love them both. Still, this place wasn't too bad, and the huge cookstove kept her little niche quite cozy, despite the cold of the floor.

A new man came in around Christmas, taking Tressie's mind off her friend's departure the previous week. He hailed from over Bannack way, Tressie heard someone say. Anxious to question him, she hurriedly piled fluffy sourdough biscuits on a platter and took them to his table.

"Excuse me, sir," she said, placing the platter upwind to make sure he caught the fresh aroma. Men about to be well fed were more pliant. "How long did you work in Bannack?"

"Till she begin to run out." He helped himself to a biscuit.

"Run out?"

"Hell, yes. She's been all but panned out. Figgered it was time for me to git up and dust. Some come to Alder Gulch, hit it big. Me, soon's I earn a stake I'm heading to Idaho Territory. Ever one's all but deserted them claims for up here, but I reckon they's color to find there yet."

"Did you ever meet a man called Evan Majors? Sturdy brown-haired fella with broad shoulders and big hazel eyes?

The miner squinted and dug at his dirty beard with black fingernails. He appeared to still be thinking as he poked his stew-filled spoon into a hidden opening in the grubby hair on his face. "No'm, can't reckon I did. But they's lots of miners wandering around. Some ain't much miners, either, don't know a shovel from a rocker." He slapped the table to loud guffaws. "For ever one who strikes, they's a hunnerd go away empty-fisted. Reckon I could have some more of that stew?"

Tressie took his bowl. "And you're sure you never run across a man name of Majors."

"Could be, but I don't recollect."

Tressie hustled away, gravely disappointed.

The gold had panned out in Bannack? Where would Papa have gone from there?

That night Caleb awoke her, coughing deep down in his throat. By morning he was running a fever and turning nearly purple with fits of coughing.

"It's the croup," Tressie told Lincolnshire, who daily stepped into the kitchen for a few words with her.

He peered at the red-faced child. "I don't know. Looks and sounds bad to me. Maybe you ought to take him down to the doctor. There's a new healing man in town, seems to be the talk of the place. I'll send someone to bring him up here. That'd be best."

Tressie felt a deep-seated fear growing inside her belly until she quivered with dread. She propped Caleb over her shoulder, which seemed the only way he could get his breath between choking spells. She cooked breakfast that way, stirring the heavy pots of mush and pans of fatback and dipping the helpings out with one hand. The men, exhausted by fighting the brutal subzero weather while working the sluices, took pity on her plight and helped themselves to coffee and seconds on the mush.

The ill-fitting boots Tressie had bought in town when the weather had turned nasty dragged heavily at her heels as she paced back and forth near the stove. She crooned and cried, beside herself with worry. "Oh, Caleb, sweet, sweet child. Don't die, please God, don't let my baby die."

She told herself it was only, after all, the croup. All babies had that in the winter, didn't they? And if she had some of Grammy's plasters she could steam it right out of him. She hoped the fancy town doctor knew those cures and would come real soon to administer some. Where in these godforsaken mountains would they find comfrey for cough syrup, or mustard for plaster? That would break up Caleb's congestion right away.

After she cleared the breakfast things, she put on a wrap and stood outside in the brittle cold. Caleb had exhausted himself and slept fitfully in his bed, propped up by a pillow to ease his breathing. After a while a large black buggy arrived pulled by a big-footed dray, and she tried to see the man hidden under the shadows of its top. Jarrad Lincolnshire caught her attention when he rode up astride his shaggy red gelding just behind the doctor. Rather than send someone else, he'd gone himself. She felt a flutter of fondness for the odd man, despite his dishonest intentions toward her friend Rose.

As Jarrad dismounted, a huge man unfolded himself from the buggy's seat. Both were bundled against the bitter wind so that only their eyes showed. She couldn't remember ever seeing a bigger man than this doctor, unless it would be Dooley Kling. She pushed away any thought of Caleb's father and scurried inside ahead of the two men.

Bending over the sick child, she touched his cheek with her own. The boy was burning up. She noted the wheeze deep in his chest and turned frightened eyes in the direction of the doctor. The bear of a man took his time unwrapping himself from an enormous buffalo-robe coat.

"He has such a high fever, Doctor. And his breathing is rattly. I'm so afraid he—"

The man's brittle stare caught at her, held on for a brief moment, and she gasped. She knew those eyes! She scanned the other features. Brashly sculpted into sharp planes, the bones of his cheeks and nose were like granite, reminding her of someone. She studied the clean-shaven features, the sand-colored hair cut neatly away from his ears and up off his white shirt collar. She shook her head and pinched at her temples with thumb and fingers. She was mistaken. Such foolishness came from worrying over the baby, she decided.

Caleb choked and gasped, causing Tressie to forget her wandering suppositions. "Tressie, this is Dr. Abel Gideon. I told you about him."

The big man nodded and said, "So this is the young fellow who's in dire straits. We'll soon have him fit again. Now, ma'am, if you'll just move aside and let me examine him."

She hovered nearby, Lincolnshire holding her arm in his long fingers as if she needed his support. Gideon was so large he blocked out all view of what he was doing as he worked over Caleb, who gasped for breath between hoarse screams.

After what seemed an endless wait, Gideon finally turned from the child. "I've given him something to purge the poison. After he's cleaned out proper, give him this."

From his bag he produced a bottle of brown liquid. "It's nasty stuff." The doctor actually chortled gruffly. "If it doesn't taste bad, it can't be good medicine."

She glared unforgivingly up at the insensitive doctor.

In return, Gideon slapped his massive girth with the flat of one hand. "Yes, well, he'll take it if you pour a few drops over sugar. Do that every four hours and make sure he drinks a lot of water."

"He won't eat," Tressie said with a quiver in her voice.

Gideon's glance shifted to her breasts in a flicker she barely noticed. "Do you need some relief?"

"Me? I'm not sick."

"The milk, I mean. Surely if he's not suckling…"

She could have sworn the man leered and reached for her bosom. The feeling was so real she took a couple of steps backward. What was it about this giant that so disturbed her? For God's sake, he was a doctor, here to heal. Hadn't Jarrad said he had a good reputation in Virginia City?

For some reason she couldn't fathom, she decided not to explain her situation to this man. It was really none of his business. Instead she merely turned away. Let him take her actions for whatever he wanted.

He laid a heavy hand on her shoulder. "Forgive me, ma'am, for being forward. I understand. But if you do need relief—for the child may not nurse for several days yet—I'll be glad to assist."

Tressie kept her back to Gideon until she heard him rustling into the heavy coat. "Plenty of water, now. That's very important. And keep him wrapped and near the stove to sweat out the fever. Don't let a breath of night air on him. It could be his death."

Tressie nodded. She could well remember Grammy cautioning about the dangers of night air, and it eased her mind to hear the same warning coming from this doctor. Perhaps he was as good as they said. She looked at him and asked, "How much do I owe you?"

Lincolnshire said, "It's okay, Tressie. I took care of the doctor."

"You can't pay my bills," she said rather sharply.

"We'll take care of it next pay period, child. I wouldn't think of paying your bills. You just stop fussing and take care of the wee mite. I'm going to get one of the men to help out here in the kitchen. You just tell him what to do and he'll do it. We've fewer mouths to feed, at any rate. How'll that be?"

Tears filled her eyes. Lincolnshire being so kind when she was so near collapse from work and worry touched her heart deeply.

While bundling Caleb into the quilt, she was struck with a vivid memory of Reed Bannon, gazing out at her from down in those soft dark eyes, saying, "You're sure something, Tressie, girl."

She buried her nose in the bundle and felt the heat emanating from the sick child's body. "No, I'm not, Reed Bannon, I'm surely not."

In her concern about survival, Tressie hadn't let herself think much on Reed. But now thoughts of him washed over her unbidden, right along with the sad realization that he was never coming back to her. She knew that with a sudden certainty that made the baby's illness that much more threatening to her sanity. First Papa, then Mama and the baby and now Reed. All had deserted her. She had nobody. Nobody but this tiny child, and she so feared he would not live.

Nothing Doc Gideon did for Caleb seemed to help. She tasted the strange brown medicine, but it wasn't comfrey. Caleb vomited and voided his bowels so many times after the doctor left that Tressie just knew there could be nothing left in the child's system. But that's what the doctor had intended.

Two, three, four times she heated water and washed the soiled clothing, bedding, and diapers. A clothesline behind the stove hung full constantly.

It was a nightmare that she prayed to be over. The baby's wrenching cough continued, and it tore at Tressie's heart. She'd get a teaspoon of water down him, only to have it come back up. He screamed until it seemed he would choke to death. She couldn't bear his suffering, and so continued to carry him over her shoulder, bundled in blankets. When not coughing, he wheezed and rattled down deep in his chest.

Lincolnshire sent word to the Golden Sun that Tressie needed someone to help out. Though a young miner lent a hand with the cooking, Tressie hadn't slept or eaten in days. Several of Rose's girls set up shifts, over Tressie's objections, to care for Caleb so she could get some rest. But Caleb only wanted his mother, and so they soon gave up. Tressie missed her friend Rose sorely, longed for her restful presence.

Doc Gideon came every evening, but Tressie could tell he knew less about what to do for her child than she herself did.

Jarrad Lincolnshire came to Tressie on the morning of the third day of Caleb's illness, sat on a crate near the hot stove, and drank a cup of coffee. Tressie knew he had something to say, feared that he would be firing her.

Instead, he said, "There's another doctor in town. A homeopath name of Dr. Monroe. Perhaps we should get him up here to take a look at the wee lad." He placed the empty tin cup on the corner of the great cast-iron stove and studied her with soulful eyes. "You yourself are looking quite peaked. Are you getting any rest at all?"

She waved a hand at him and shifted Caleb to her left shoulder. He dragged in a great wheezing breath, whimpered, and grew quiet. "It's not me, it's my baby. He's not getting any better. The purging is only making him weaker. The fever comes and goes. And all the man does is poke and prod around on him and give him more of that bitter medicine. I don't think I can stand much more, and neither can Caleb. What is a homeopath?"

"I don't suppose I'm quite sure, but many of our townfolk swear by the man. He preaches cleanliness and the proper food. Says humans can't live like this, all shoved together without proper—uh—sanitary facilities."

Tears formed in Tressie's eyes. Eyes that gritted with weariness and threatened to fall shut at any moment. "Cleanliness is next to godliness," she murmured, and sagged back against the counter at her back.

She felt strong arms supporting her, guiding her to her cot, but she still wouldn't give up the baby. "Fetch this doctor for me, please," she whispered to Lincolnshire. "Someone has to help Caleb. If he dies, I can't go on. Please save my baby."

In a dark haze Tressie cradled Caleb, rocking back and forth monotonously, unaware that Lincolnshire had gone to bring back Dr. Monroe. Her next conscious act was that of trying to keep someone from taking Caleb away from her. A face, round and red-cheeked, hovered over her, his soft hands pressing her to lie back on the cot and pulling a quilt up over her exhausted body. The doctor had Caleb now. He would make him well.

She spiraled into a well of dark mystery. A place where Reed dwelled, waiting for her.

Telling her he hadn't really ever deserted her, but had always been there watching over her and Caleb. And she screamed at him to leave her be. To stop fooling with her. It hurt so much to love a man who could do such a dreadful thing. Just like Papa. He came, too, laughing and calling her his sweet little honey. The pain and anguish ripped at her. Too much to bear, losing them all.

Take me, too, God. Take me, too, she cried.

Once she opened her eyes and thought she saw Reed,

hovering over her, touching her cheek with icy fingers. "Oh, Reed, our baby," she whimpered. 'Take care of our baby." He didn't reply, and when she awoke again, daylight had come and she was alone. Alone like before, alone like always.

The empty mess tent was deathly still except for the snapping and whipping of the canvas in the brutal howling wind. She moaned and rolled over, dropping her hand off the edge of the mattress to touch Caleb, who was sleeping in his crate beside the bed. The crate wasn't there; nor was her baby.

A dreadful melancholy filled her, and she felt as if she had been immersed in a tank of icy water. "Nooooo," she howled, raising herself and fighting a wave of nausea and dizziness, her cry a thin wail of despair. "Where's my baby? I want my baby."

She was finally able to swing her legs off the bed and settle both feet on the dirt floor, only to find someone had removed her shoes. She still wore heavy wool socks over cotton stockings; her woolen skirt was twisted up around her waist to reveal unbleached muslin pantaloons.

Shakily, she came to her feet. A wrap was draped over the crate in which Caleb should be sleeping, and she grabbed it up. The mess tent was empty. Tressie staggered toward the doors, pushed her way through, and gasped.

The brutal cold sucked her breath from her lungs, leaving only brittle emptiness. She could see nothing but a wall of white. Snow blew thick in the air; it covered the ground and drifted around the huge tent until she stood knee-deep in the stuff. Pulling the wrap up over her head and clutching it at her breasts, she battled her way through the snow, feet growing absolutely numb after only two or three steps. She drew the wrap over her mouth and took shallow breaths to fight the fiery spasms of pain in her lungs.

Where is everybody? The words froze before they left her mouth. Turning to go back into the tent, she discovered that it had disappeared behind her. She was left stranded and alone, completely surrounded by a world that had gone deathly white.

Tears of distress turned to icicles on her cheeks. Where was her baby? Where was everyone? Why had they left her all alone?

'Tressie? Tressie, are you there?" A voice that was only an echo bounded on the vicious wind.

"Help! Help me!"

The vision wrapped in furs came out of nowhere, slammed into her in his haste, then caught her by the shoulders. A tall and sweetly familiar figure whose name she couldn't think of at all.

Lincolnshire lifted her into the blessed warmth of his fur-robed body. "What in God's name are you doing wandering around in this blizzard? Come back inside where it's warm."

Tressie lost all control over the sounds that boiled from deep inside her. Wet explosions of incoherent pleas. In her mind, she knew what she said, but could not herself understand the words that came from her mouth.

"Someone's taken my baby. Caleb. I have to find him. Please save me, save Caleb. Don't let him die, too. I have to take care of him. I have to look for Papa...and Reed ...and Caleb. Ooooh, please."

She pummeled her rescuer with cold-numbed fists as he carried her back inside.

How could she explain the baby's death to Papa? She would never forgive him for letting Mama and the baby die. For making her bury them out on the plains where the rain and wind and sun and snow could get to them. Their flesh, their very being. "Why did you leave me? Why did everyone leave me?" she cried into the damp, musky-smelling fur. "Oh, God, I'm sorry, sorry, sorry."

She was afraid to let go of this man who cradled her like a child, rescued her from the cold.

She feared she would fly away into that ugly black hole that seemed the only safe place to be now. Sudden warmth washed over her; hands chafed at her feet, then at her hands. They laid her back and covered her up to her chin. She dozed. It was not yet time to awake and face the terrible reality she feared awaited her.

All too soon someone shook at her shoulder, touched her cheek, called her name so that she was forced to open her eyes. She looked up into the kind face of the homeopathic doctor she barely remembered. "Lord, you gave us all such a fright."

"Where's Caleb? Where's my baby?"

Another face appeared, far above that of Dr. Monroe. The long and lean-jawed Jarrad Lincolnshire. "My dear child, you could have died out there. Whatever were you thinking of?"

Neither of them had answered her question. With frightened eyes she watched each in turn. Something terrible had happened to Caleb, and they weren't going to tell her. Filled with a deep and abiding anguish from which she feared she would never recover, she began to cry.

Two

Reed was thinking of Tressie when the band of Crow rode out of the sun, whooping madly, their ponies' tails flaring like banners. Even when standing flat-footed on a windless day, he'd never been much of a marksman. Atop a freight load on a careening wagon, he'd be lucky if he could hit sky. But he damned well better try. Reed belly-crawled toward the rear of the bouncing wagon and aimed the Henry from a crouch. Dismissing memories of Tressie bathing naked in the early dawn, he pulled off a dozen shots into the twenty or so charging savages. Six braves tumbled into the churning dust.

The Henry repeating rifle, even with its drawbacks, was a wonder indeed. Firing a few more rounds in rapid succession, he shouted a war whoop of his own, and the remaining braves split in two groups, coming up on both sides of the wagon. Reed countered by scrabbling backward into the seat beside Chim, using the freight as a shield against a rain of flying arrows while he reloaded.

Old Chim lashed out at the mules, but they were giving everything they had, the wagon rattling and banging and shaking along the rutted trail. Reed raised his head to see the two groups gaining. One young brave had actually leaped from his horse, to catch the lashing across the freight and spring to the top of the load. Reed aimed and fired twice. The brave, whose eyes Reed saw clearly at the moment he squeezed the trigger, toppled backward right under the hooves of one of the Indian ponies. Feet tangled up in the fallen brave, the pony and its rider somersaulted.

Reed rose to his knees and fired rapidly, swinging the barrel of the gun as he did so. He counted three mounted braves when the band reined up and let the wagon go.

He wanted not to think of the thing he had just done. Killing always left a bad taste. So he thought instead that they'd nearly bought it that time, him and the old man. He shifted to a sitting position on the seat beside Chim.

The driver hadn't slowed down the stampeding mules, giving them one hell of a wild ride.

Maybe he didn't realize the Indians had given up.

Reed glanced in his direction, intending to tell him, but instead muttered, "Aw, hell, Chim," and touched the slumped shoulders. An arrow had caught the old man in the back, midway down his left side. Angled like it was, and him bent forward to urge on the team, sure as hell it had pierced his heart.

Reed stowed the Henry and laced the reins through his own fingers. Bracing his boots on the footboard, he hauled back, feeling the muscles in his back and shoulders bunch in protest.

"Whoa, there. Whoa, you ornery devils," he yelled.

The body of the driver bounced like a rag doll. Reed went for the brake, the mules slowed and finally came to a halt. Old Chim slid sideways and would have fallen to the ground if Reed hadn't dropped the reins and caught at the old man's arm.

"Aw, hell, Chim," he repeated holding the lolling head against his shoulder.

He and Chim had established a friendship of sorts, neither talking much, but exchanging some innermost feelings nevertheless. Reed would miss the old codger, who had been as tough as a saddle when it came to handling a team of stubborn mules. He had a muleskinner's philosophy about life, too, and it had been his words, though he would never know it, that kept Reed from riding to St. Louis and insisting the Army punish him for his earlier lapse.

He'd told his tale to Chim about a month after they started hauling freight together for the Dacota Company. To Reed, getting the horse-stealing incident off his chest became more necessary as time passed. He wanted to go to Tressie, but not carrying that kind of baggage.

The banty-legged muleskinner had grinned up at Reed. "'Tarnation, boy. If they was to hang ever man who run from that war, or shot a damn Yankee in the process, they wouldn't be enough rope in all the Americas, and most certain not airy enough trees. As for stealing a horse, hell, you're half Indian, ain't you? Means you jest plain didn't know no better."

Chim had chuckled and spat into the dust then, casting Reed a knowing look with squinted eyes.

Busy strapping the driver's body down for the ride to the post at Powder River, he remembered that and other similar conversations. Chim had been a good friend. Once they reached the post, he would notify the freightmaster for the company and see what they wanted him to do with the rest of this load consigned to the Bighorn River trading post.

The small Dacota Company ran three mule-drawn freight wagons out of Julesburg down on the Platte River. This one followed the Bozeman Trail, supplying the growing network of trading posts as far as the Yellowstone River. There were plans to extend the run into the gold strike country over Alder Gulch way, and that's why Reed had opted for riding gun on this one. He might be ready to head for Virginia City come spring, and what better way to go than doing a job he was being paid for. Another arm of the Dacota freight line ran the

Platte River Road to Denver, and the third followed the North Platte over Rattlesnake Pass to supply trading posts scattered through the area. He wouldn't have had that run for all the gold in Oregon Territory, for on that treacherous trip a guard and driver were killed an average of once a week.

The larger freight companies traveled in caravans and used oxen to pull the loaded wagons.

They were less apt to lose men to Indian attacks, for they could circle up at night and form a miniature fort. But he wasn't a bullwhacker—a job that took immense cunning. It was said some could flick a fly off a bull's ear without ever touching the beast with the eighteen-foot-long whip. He had no desire to be around those big dumb oxen for any reason. All he'd manage to do with that whip was put out his own eye. Besides, big companies tended to hire experienced men.

He'd got on with Dacota because they were a small independent with some firm contracts, several oversized buckboard wagons, and a desperate need for help. Unlike most mule trains, whose drivers rode the left wheeler animal—one of twelve—rather than the wagon, Dacota kept it cheap and simple. They put a driver and a guard up top, the freight covered with canvas and tied down behind. Now that Chim was dead, he was afraid the company would cancel this run through the months of January and February, what with the snow so deep to boot. There'd even been talk the owners were thinking of selling out to the giant of western freighting, Russell, Majors & Waddell out of Leavenworth, Kansas.

At the moment he had more to worry about than rumors. He seated himself beside the lashed-down body, pulled on Chim's heavy gloves, and once again took up the leather reins. Slapping them briskly, he set the animals to moving. The wagon rolled forward in jerks and fits, finally picking up speed as the mules hit their stride.

At the post Reed told his story, then waited in the small Dacota office, hat in hand, for the verdict.

"We ain't got no choice," freightmaster Cord Wiggett squeaked. He was small in stature with a tinny voice, a bald head, and the roundest baby face Reed had ever seen on a full-grown man.

Reed bunched the gloves in one hand. "But I'm not a driver. I rode shotgun."

The little man balled his fists on the scarred wooden desk. "You want to keep your job, don't you?"

Reed nodded and sighed, giving over reluctantly. "I'll not go into Powder River country without a guard, job or no. Get me a marksman to watch our back and I'll do it."

If it wasn't the Arapaho on the warpath it was the Blackfoot or Crow, with an occasional Sioux band joining in. Reed couldn't blame them much. Watching the white man swarm all over their land was surely a mite fearsome.

He'd probably be right there among them had he stayed with his mother's people. Killing white men along with the rest. Likely he'd have been a mite more accurate with bow and arrow than he was with a rifle.

By dawn the next morning, Reed found himself back up on the wagon seat. He dragged in a long breath and slapped the broad leather reins over the backs of the mule team.

Seated beside him was a young sharpshooter who went by the name of Brett Scoggins. He was as eager as a pup and just about as clumsy, his feet and hands being sized way too big for his compact body. But the boy could hit anything he could see with his sparkling blue eyes, and he saw a far piece. He carried a cud of tobacco in one cheek and already his teeth were staining brown. He couldn't be over eighteen, Reed had decided after watching him stumble all over himself climbing aboard. It wasn't long before he found he preferred driving to banging around on his backside with both eyes peeled in all directions at once.

He deeply regretted having sent Tressie and Caleb to Virginia City alone. But he still didn't see how he could have done any different. He was haunted now with fears of her fate. Damn it, why couldn't he just have hooked up with her? Her vengeful notions and Reed's own past be gone to hell.

The boy was blathering on, something about Quantrill's latest activities. Reed pulled himself away from fond memories of sun-splashed hair and spring-green eyes, the warm softness of rosy-tipped breasts. This kind of dreaming could get a fellow in deep trouble.

"What'd you say, Scoggins?"

"I just asked if you'd heard about Quantrill."

"You mean Lawrence? Yeah. That was a long while back."

'Yeah, but then they raided Baxter Springs, Kansas. Killed sixty-five Union soldiers."

Reed shrugged. Killing soldiers was war, pure and simple, the way he looked at it. Now, that thing in Lawrence, all those women and babies, that was shameful, and he would be forever grateful he'd left that bunch before they got started on such as that.

"Rumor is they're headed for Kentucky to regroup. Hope they don't do no killing down there."

"Why should they? They're Rebs through and through."

The boy snorted. "The hell they are. They ain't nothing but a bunch a outlaws, and ought to be hung out to dry. Skinned alive."

Reed twitched his lips into a smile. The boy was obviously repeating what he'd heard around Fort Laramie from the soldiers there, who for the most part champed at the bit to be involved in the war and resented having to police the frontier. They made up for it by jawing. Still, Reed didn't much like this talk. If someone ever came along who could tie him in to that bunch of border raiders, he could well be hung himself.

Out here in the territories, law was a sometime thing, mostly carried out by bands of vigilantes who dealt out swift justice at the end of a rope draped over the nearest tree. They didn't ask a whole lot of questions, either.

Brett poked Reed with the butt of his rifle, startling him out of his reverie. "Hey, I asked what's your hurry?"

"Huh?" Reed dragged his attention back to the job at hand to see that the mules were galloping flat out, their long ears laid back in protest. He eased back on the poor beasts. Best not to wreck a wagonload of this size. The trail was hazardous enough in such weather, though traffic did keep the ice chewed up so traction came better.

He caught up with a stagecoach toward midday and the two traveled together till dark, when they reached a rest stop where both could lay out a few hours. He left his companion unhitching the mules and went inside to fetch coffee. He and Chim would have made camp, but Reed saw no need here. He and the boy would bed down under the wagon, but they might as well take a meal from the station master. Inside the cramped log cabin, he hung back until the stage passengers were served. There was a woman among them, and Reed studied her intently.

She looked exhausted, beaten down by the trip. He couldn't help but wonder what a woman was doing in this punishing country. She'd be worn out and dead before she reached forty, he'd allow. How was life treating Tressie and the baby? He hoped they had found work and shelter.

Tucked into the simple fare, he boy had little to say for which he was grateful. Rolled up in blankets and canvas on the cold hard ground long silences as were common in the mountain wilderness, filled up easily with unwanted thoughts.

Suppose men had taken advantage of Tressie. Closing his eyes, he was beset with visions of her gentle beauty ravaged by some brutal man...or worse, men. God, how could he have been so callous? He should have remained with her, protected her, loved her.

Reed muttered aloud and turned over. Beside him Brett grunted and shifted to settle close, sharing the warmth. When Reed finally did fall asleep, he dreamed of Tressie, but every time he reached out for her, she drifted off, trailing a sharp laugh that grated painfully in his ears. He awoke shivering from the cold and his regrets.

Both drivers decided to keep the two rigs together, Reed bringing up the rear, until they reached the trading post on the Powder River. Such a joining would double their chances of getting through in one piece.

When they reached the Bighorn Mountains, the traveling group discovered that snow had drifted along the trail until it touched the horses' bellies. The coach soon bogged down. Reed halted the team of mules, looped the handful of reins over the brake handle, and jumped down. A few miles back he'd tied his hat down with a woolen neck scarf and donned a buffalo-hide coat, for the temperature had been dropping all day. He felt much like one of the large animals himself as he plowed his way forward to the stranded coach.

Liberty McFee, a scabrous but competent driver whom Reed had met on previous occasions, was already down surveying the situation. Canvas sashes had been drawn over all the stage windows, but when Reed passed the coach, one lifted at the corner. He caught the glance of a pair of feminine eyes. Their look of fear clutched at his gut. He didn't even know if the lady on board was accompanied by someone or had come alone, but he experienced a sharp twinge of sympathy for her. Such a predicament was bad enough for a man. How must she feel? How must Tressie have felt when he bade her good-bye and walked away? He turned, wanting to reassure the woman, but she had lowered the flap. The door opened and three men crawled down, capturing his attention.

For a long while the men stood around, hip deep in the powdery snow, and contemplated various solutions.

Liberty scratched at his bearded chin. "Didn't have a lady aboard, I'd say dig in for the night, but it's only a few miles yonder to a rest stop. I'd sure like to git her there." He squinted up into the bright white sky. "'Sides, I'd say we're in for another snow come nightfall. Hell, we could be here till spring thaw. I say let's walk 'em out if we kin."

Reed eyed the snowfield completely obliterating the trail. Up ahead lay a sharp curve around a rocky outcropping, then the trail wound into the lee of the mountain. These drifts out here in the open ought to give way in the cut where the wind should have swept the snow away.

"I'm with you, Liberty. We can make it around the bend into that draw, it ought to be clear. I'll unhitch the mules and lead 'em. With nothing to pull, them lop- eared stubborn sons a bitches can wade anything. We'll break trail, then come back doing the same. We should then be able to pull both the coach and the wagon through. And if not, we'll carry your passengers into a more sheltered place to bed down for the night."

Everyone agreed, Liberty adding with a chuckle that if those six runt mules couldn't break trail alone, he'd unhitch the horses, too. It didn't take long for Reed and Brett to unhitch the mules. Reed walked behind, urging the team through the deep snow. He left Brett on the wagon seat to keep an extra eye out for marauders, though in this weather he didn't expect any trouble unless it be from wildcat or bear, both of which preferred the long shadows of evening.

Reed couldn't help thinking of the woman on board the stage. Her presence continued to take his mind back to Tressie Majors. Why, when he finally did meet a woman he could truly be happy with, did everything have to be so troublesome? Life sometimes was mighty wearisome. Just thinking about her, what with all this frigid weather, made his gut ache and his manhood hard as a damn icicle. Tough as life was on this relentless frontier, a man needed a woman to bed down with, a woman who could keep him warm and cozy and satisfied. Lord, how good it would feel....

The mules rounded the outcropping in their relentless single-minded way and broke from the deep drifts onto frozen ground swept clean by wind, just as Reed had said. Relieved, he hauled back on the team, shouting, "Whoa, you ornery cusses."

By damn, he'd been right. The storm had bellowed its way right up this draw and blown all the snow out into the open, leaving the trail as slick as a skinned possum. And in the quiet of the cold afternoon, he made out a tall plume of smoke rising from a chimney hidden in a grove of enormous pines up ahead. They would make it.

With the already frigid temperature plunging, it was decided everyone would spend the night inside the station. The mules and horses were put up in a lean-to and fed. Reed, Brett, and Liberty completed that chore. The storm Liberty had predicted earlier stirred noisily, then blasted down out of the Bighorns with a ferocity unknown by flat- landers.

Crammed in the small log dwelling, one woman and nine men huddled as close to the fireplace and as far from the walls as possible. While the wind careened and blasted at the structure with a vengeance, they all tried to sleep, propped against each other for warmth and because there wasn't room for all to lie down. When dawn awoke them, they found they were stranded. Drifts all but covered the log cabin, and it took most of the morning to tunnel a path from the door to the attached lean-to and feed the animals.

Brett took it upon himself to see to the only female among

them. It was touching to watch him arrange private facilities for her needs and stand guard at the blanket-draped corner.

The blizzard blew itself out late that afternoon and just at sunset, a flare of golden light blazed across the pristine world. Reed stood shoulder-deep in the dug-out path, having come from haying the animals, and gazed in wonder at such a sight. He had never seen anything quite so breathtaking as the snow-covered ragged mountain peaks reflected in shards of brilliant orange and pink light. Such virgin beauty brought a huge lump to his throat and filled him with a yearning that stung at his eyes.

Dear God, would he never find a home and hearth?

The Indians came the next afternoon, one riding in slowly, the others hanging back. The single brave, whose pony plowed relentlessly through the snow, looked gaunt. Reed stepped out, holding the Henry loosely in one hand so the brave could see he had it, but wasn't pointing it.

Not yet. The small band looked cold and hungry and, if no one started anything, would probably go away if given food.

The proud Dakota Sioux dismounted with agility, paying no attention to the snow. He wore a buffalo robe around his shoulders, and hide boots. Touching his chest, he told Reed his name was Eagle That Hunts.

Reed touched the flat of one hand to his own chest and uttered for the first time in almost fifteen years his own Sioux name. The action surprised even himself. He thought he might have forgotten how to say Wolf Who Runs in Sioux, but the syllables rolled off his tongue sweet and clear.

With a look of pleasure on his regal features, the brave said, "We came looking for food. Your smoke brought us." The man touched the side of his nose and sniffed.

Reed nodded. "What little we have, we'll share with you. There are many of us inside."

The brave immediately caught the subtlety and cast a

quick glance over his shoulder. At a border of tall pines, where wind had swept the snow clear, eight braves sat their ponies. Reed thought he saw the stock of a rifle but couldn't be sure, they were so far away.

He held up a hand. "One minute. I'll pack something," he said, and backed through the door, closing it swiftly.

"What do they want?" Liberty asked.

"They're hungry. Look half starved." Reed shook his head. "I don't know. We can share with them, and they might just decide to kill us and take it all, or they might go away. If we don't offer anything at all, they'll for sure kill us and take it. But it ain't mine to offer. I just vote to give the poor souls some food. This I know for sure: They're hungrier than we are."

A couple of the male passengers murmured in agreement, but two others, who looked pretty wild to Reed, objected. "Hell, I say we shoot the sons a bitches. Among us we got enough guns. Why should we give them food? Blamed red savages."

The other nodded, then took another tack. "How do you know how to palaver with them redskinned no-goods, anyway? I ain't sure we should give a breed a vote in this anyways."

Liberty, usually quiet but easy to rile, hefted his rifle, a well-worn Springfield.

"Hold up, hoss. We ain't having any of that fighting amongst ourselves. We all get a vote in this, and that's 'cause I and this here gun say so. This feller is right, and he knows. We got a fifty-fifty chance if we share, none at all if we don't. They'll just wait till dark and burn us out. Hell, they ain't fools to ride in against armed men holed up like we are."

The woman made a soft sound down in her throat and Brett patted her arm. "We do need to think of the lady and what's best for her," the boy said.

One of the wild ones guffawed. "We all know what's best for wimmen."

Brett launched himself on the fellow, who shook him off like a pesky fly. He fetched up on the floor with the woman kneeling beside him.

Reed stepped in. "Fighting among ourselves won't solve our problem. And they aren't going to wait forever for a decision. Do we give them some food or not?"

The man who had knocked Brett to the floor made a move so quick and unexpected that no matter how Reed thought about it later, he didn't see how he or Liberty could have stopped him. Bulling his way through to the door, he jerked it open, lifted his rifle, and shot the unsuspecting brave who waited beside his pony.

Reed launched himself against the shooter, but too late to help their situation. He had been right about seeing a rifle, for a shot rang out almost immediately, and the bullet cut a chunk of wood from a log just above where he grappled with the other man. No one had to urge either of them back inside.

The Indians attacked late that evening, waiting until deep blue and purple shadows crept across the glistening snow.

Reed had gone to feed the animals when he heard the commotion. By then it was too late. Several of the raiding band had cut through the low roof and, once inside the cabin, made quick work of their massacre. Several shots were fired and the woman screamed, an unholy sound that was cut off abruptly.

He had his Henry, and he managed to pick off a couple of the braves as they came for the horses, but then they were on him. Why they didn't kill him, Reed never knew. But he came to his senses half frozen and thinking he'd gone blind, for it was as dark as the hubs of hell when he dragged his eyes open.

As he scrambled and fought to rise, he discovered he was covered with snow. Frantically he searched for a way out, digging with hands that were numb with cold. Then she came to him, in a vision as clear and plain as if she were really kneeling over him.

And she reached out her hand, touched his cheek, her green eyes flashing with great spirit. Her fragrance washed around him; her passion-filled him with warmth.

He shook free of the snow and climbed to his feet, stumbling a few steps before righting himself. Reaching out to embrace her, he almost wept when he saw that she had gone.

A quivering deep down in his gut told him he was on the verge of freezing to death, and he hugged his arms tightly around his own middle. No matter what was inside that cabin, he had to go there or die.

Somewhere off in the distance a wolf howled, sending a fresh spate of shivers through him.

He got his bearings, at last able to see in the reflection of starshine on the white world around him. The Indians had taken all the animals; they would probably eat the mules. He started toward the station, dragging one hand over the high ridge of snow alongside the path. The nearer he got to the cabin, the more he dreaded going inside. But he had no choice.

The smell of death hung hot and brackish, though it was as cold inside the cabin as out.

Reed built up a fire quickly, then set to his grisly task. He knew he would never forget the sight that greeted him there, and for the first time in his life was glad for his experiences in the war. This task was made a little easier for it; not much, but a little. Even at that, he was sobbing by the time he dragged out the last body. For it was that of the woman, and she had been shot in the temple. Brett had protected her to the last. Poor kid, poor damned brave kid.

With tears freezing on his cheeks, Reed covered them all over with snow, not knowing anything else to do. Back inside, he discovered the lump on his head and the blood that had dried over the back of his coat. More hungry than vicious, the Dakota had hit and run fast, settling for the horses and leaving Reed for dead without bothering to finish him off.

Well, perhaps they had been right. He was probably as good as dead stranded out here in the middle of the winter with no food or a mount. But he had traveled afoot before, half starved and beaten, and by God, he could do it again.

By morning he had burned every shattered stick of furniture in the place along with a great deal of the wood supply stacked in one corner. But even a huge roaring fire couldn't keep the demons at bay, and that night Reed was faced with some of the worst demons of his entire twenty-six years.

They attacked from every dark and dreadful corner of the scene of this slaughter. The young boys who defended their homes and their women against armies from both sides of the brutal war. The dead and dying from the battlefields. The brave Indians he had fought alongside at Pea Ridge, who had died for a way of life they didn't even understand. Doomed from the outset, the red man took sides when in reality he should have been defending his own right to the land where white men spilled each other's blood. And as if that weren't enough, Reed's guilt over sending Tressie and the boy away alone grew into the most formidable demon of them all. He loved her with all his heart, and he couldn't have her, but that was no excuse for what he had done.

Well, he didn't care anymore whether she could be his or not. He was going to her, and no matter what happened, he would be with her. Chances were no one would ever come to the frontier looking for a no-account deserter and thief. Even so, all he knew was that he had lived for a reason, and it wasn't to wander around lonely and bereft seeking something he might never find. What he really needed he'd already found, and like an idiot let it go.

He scarcely slept. At first light, he set out to salvage what he could. The Indians had ransacked the cabin, taking all the food and clothing. They'd stolen the animals. But they hadn't even bothered with the freight wagon. Reed could hardly believe that, but supposed that in all the excitement they hadn't seen it nosed in behind the stagecoach back in the trees. It had been nearly dark. Whatever the reason, he was able to dig out enough food and clothing to suffice.

As prepared as he could be, Reed took one final long look at the cabin, and began the treacherous walk out.

Three

The last day of March in the gold town of Virginia City, Montana Territory, Tressie could taste spring, smell it in the bite of afternoon breezes, feel it on her skin so that she experienced sudden urges to strip out of her long johns and woolens. The morning dawned clear and brittle. The deep snow, previously frozen so hard horses walked on top of it, glittered with moisture.

The path to the mess tent, with shoulder-high banks of winter-long snow, turned slushy underfoot during daylight hours. It wasn't warm yet, but it soon would be. That evening of this perfect final day of March, Lincolnshire set out to coax her into accompanying him on the half-mile ride into town the next day.

"Just what you need, child," he told her, presenting the idea as she prepared supper for the crew.

She lifted her shoulders and sighed. "I'm content here. I don't want to go anywhere. There's nothing wrong with that, is there?"

He held up broad palms. "I know, I know. You're perfectly all right. That's precisely why you don't speak for days on end, nor eat, either, for that matter. You're a walking-around skeleton. What you need is some female company and a shopping trip. Surely you have accumulated some funds. Where would you have spent anything?"

She couldn't help but grin at his manner and hold up both

hands in supplication. "I give up, I'll go to town. Anything to get you to stop blathering at me. You sound just like my father used to when I'd misbehaved and was pouting over my punishment. I'm really fine. It's just hard, that's all, getting over…"

The words choked off, and she couldn't go on, couldn't yet speak of Caleb, whose tiny body lay in the cold of the storage tent not fifty yards from where she and Lincolnshire talked.

It was almost too much to bear, thinking of the chubby, brown-skinned child she had loved with all her heart and who was now forever lost to her. She was never to hear his laughter, or see him walk and talk and call her mommy. Too soon the ground would soften and she'd have to bid a last farewell to the child she would never see grow up. For come spring thaw, those who hadn't made it through the harsh winter would all be buried. She attempted to soothe the heartache by imagining Caleb with Mama, frolicking in fields of daisies, flushed by a warm and constant sun in a place where she would someday join them.

Of course Lincolnshire was right that she needed a change. She just wasn't sure that a trip to Virginia City would help. Even now, after all this time, she dreamed of the day Reed Bannon would come strolling up over the rim of the hill, dark eyes dancing, and grab her up in his strong arms. Kiss away the loneliness and share her grief, take her somewhere far from this place of silenced dreams. For only the precious memories of him had kept her from dying of a broken heart during the awful months since Caleb's death.

She no longer thought of her quest to find Papa and exact revenge. Too much heartache had numbed her senses so that she wondered if she could even remember his face.

Still trying to get out of the suggested shopping trip, she protested weakly one more time. "Maggie visits sometimes. She's a friend. And soon Rose will be back from St. Louis. I'll just stay here and fix a big supper for everyone."

But nothing had worked. Just by looking at Lincolnshire she could tell she was making no headway at all. He was determined, and what was worse than a determined Englishman, she didn't know. The man always got his way without ever raising his voice even the tiniest bit. Everyone wanted to please him. It was easy to see why Rose loved this tall foreigner with the odd voice and winning ways.

The object of her contemplations propped himself on an empty wooden barrel and chewed on the end of a sulfur match. "Do you ever think of finding yourself a good man, child? There are plenty in this country who would fall all over themselves to be wed to the likes of you. All they see, after all, are girls like that Maggie. A prostitute. Most would aim higher."

Tressie swung on him, ready to do battle. "Is that how you feel about Rose, too?"

Perhaps only she understood how deeply Rose loved this aloof Englishman. He certainly had no idea. And even if he had, she wondered if that would stop him from taking advantage of that love. He had a wife and two daughters in London, and had no intentions of deserting them for a mere prostitute. Why couldn't Rose see that?

His gray eyes leveled on her. "And what would you know about Rose and me? Whatever we do, it is private, and not your concern. She does her job, that's what I pay her for, and it's nothing for you to even think about."

He paused and scuffled one booted toe smartly on the frozen floor. When he spoke again, his voice grew soft. "Now look at us, having words over such trivial things. What are you preparing for the evening meal?"

She wanted to snap at him that anything to do with Rose Langue was far from trivial, but held her tongue and turned quickly to stir at the simmering pot. "Venison stew, what else?"

She sneaked a look at Lincolnshire. Did he only miss the

beautiful blond saloon keeper in his bed, or were his earlier words of derision simply a smokescreen? She wanted to believe he held Rose in a special place in his heart, but God how fickle men could be when it came to women.

"Perhaps we can find something to add to the larder in town. Men are apt to be getting tired of deer meat. I'll take a hindquarter of venison and we'll barter, maybe come up with a freshly cured ham," Lincolnshire said. Then he unfolded his six and a half feet, slapped his thighs through layers of woolen garments, and said, "Be ready to leave right after breakfast in the morning. The men can finish off that stew for dinner tomorrow. Just put some more water in it."

The next morning she finished her chores quickly. Despite her earlier reluctance, she actually looked forward to riding into town with Lincolnshire. She laid it to the weather. Who wouldn't welcome the chance to escape this mess tent when the sun shined so gloriously?

When Lincolnshire arrived, she covered her head and shoulders with a black woolen shawl and followed him to the buggy. He helped her in and bundled her up in buffalo robes for the short trip down the side of the mountain into Virginia City.

The clever Englishman had put two men to work early in the winter constructing heavy skids for the buggy. The sled proved quite innovative and was copied quickly by several other townspeople. Soon the ground would grow too mushy, and the runners would have to be replaced with the black-and-red-spoked wheels.

Once settled in the nest of warm robes, Tressie gazed in awe at the world of glittering ice and snow. The majestic peaks skirted by gigantic pine were surely a most gorgeous sight to behold and she didn't want to miss anything. How could God have created such wonder, only to smite down an innocent child before he could enjoy that world?

Brilliant spring sunshine struck the blue-white jagged peaks, throwing spines of light in rainbow colors that changed with every shift of the sled across the icy terrain. Below, the town of Virginia City lay nested in drifts of pristine beauty that would soon give way to spring flowers.

The boardwalks had been shoveled clean, leaving doorways accessible. These brave souls who tread on new ground, regardless of the danger, had managed to dig themselves out a burrow and carry on a somewhat normal daily life in this harsh wilderness.

Why couldn't winter go on forever? Once it ended and Caleb was laid to rest her life here would truly be over. She would be free to leave. Where would she go, and what would she do? A sob escaped her lips. She could not ever be more than two or three thoughts away from Caleb's terrible death. Not even when Mama died had she felt this lonely. So soon Reed had come to fill the void. But now she had nothing. Even her only friend Rose had deserted her. What kind of life was this, anyway?

"Do you think the Overland stage is running?" she asked Lincolnshire as he drove to the livery to leave the rig.

"I've no doubt of it. They're a hardy lot, those stage drivers. Only the worst blizzards hold them up for any time at all. Them and the freighters keep the trails broken pretty good. There are so many people out here now, Tressie. My God, can you imagine a country this size being peopled from coast to coast? It absolutely boggles the mind, it does. All working and buying and eating and wearing clothing and boots and building houses. 'Tis amazing what you colonists have accomplished in this raw world."

Rather than try to make sense of what he meant by some of the things he said, she often simply listened to the eloquence of his voice and ignored the meaning of the words. This was one of those times.

The tall Englishman climbed down and went around to offer assistance. She burrowed from under the robes and took his hand.

He didn't settle for that, instead plucked her from the seat as if she were a will-o'-the-wisp. Before she could gasp, he had deposited her on the boardwalk, leaving her feeling a bit giddy.

After regaining her composure, she murmured, "Thank you," and searched for something to do or say. Heat flushed her face, the heat overpowering the cold of the day.

The blue dress she wore was of the fabric Rose had chosen on their first shopping trip together. The floral design had begun to fade, but she hadn't found the energy to care. Because the weather was still brisk, she wore woolen long johns underneath and knee-high boots over woolen socks. The shawl was draped over her pinned-up hair and around her throat. Gloves covered her small hands. Only her cheeks and eyes were exposed.

Lincolnshire held his hands at her tiny waist for a moment after settling her on the boardwalk. He regarded the gaunt loveliness of her young features with a deep sigh of longing. She reminded him a little of his youngest daughter, Leslie, and he missed his family so. Perhaps this spring he would make the long trip back to London. Try once again to convince Victoria that she and the girls would be comfortable here in this wild new country. He would build them a house such as had never been seen in this place. It would be as near to a castle as possible. He could send stonecutters into the mountains and—

He let the thoughts break off when Tressie, in an effort to turn his avid attention away from her to something else, asked, "Do you suppose they're still fighting the Civil War? How long can it go on?"

"I wouldn't care to guess, but indeed they are still fighting. Do you not look at the Post? The war still rages. And they care little for the needs of us out here in the territories. We are not in the States, after all. We live by an entirely different set of laws."

She did not read the local newspaper, had little interest in anything printed there. Before Caleb died she had enjoyed eavesdropping on the miners, listening to their talk of hangings and battles and gold strikes. She scarcely cared enough to do such a thing anymore. Consciously, she couldn't remember any specific happenings since that ugly January day when Lincolnshire had rescued her from the blizzard, only to inform her of the child's death. And her not able to ever hold his dear body in her arms ...tell him goodbye.

Lincolnshire tucked her gloved hand into the crook of his left arm and together they strolled along the boardwalk.

A price slate on the mercantile caught her eye. Flour at $27 a hundredweight and eggs at $1 each were chalked in.

"I thought things like flour and sugar were made in the East and shipped out here. Wouldn't those trading routes be affected by war?" she asked.

"We get much of our trade goods from Salt Lake City, or by boat up the river from St. Louis," he told her absently. He appeared to be paying very little attention to her. Probably thinking of Rose.

Abruptly Tressie caught sight of someone that made her jerk backward on Lincolnshire's arm and gasp. Coming toward them, seeming to take up all the width of the boardwalk, was a bear of a man wrapped to the ears in a buffalo robe.

"It can't be," she cried. "Dooley Kling?"

"Who?" her companion asked, watching the blood drain from her face, leaving her white as the snowcapped peaks.

The man came closer, and Lincolnshire nodded. "Afternoon, Doctor." Then to Tressie out of the side of his mouth, "Are you ill, child? Whatever is wrong?"

She continued to watch the mountain of a man who had lifted his bowler hat in greeting and stepped around them on the street side to go on his way.

"Oh, Lord, for a moment I thought— Who was that man?"

Lincolnshire gazed at her in concern. "Why, that was Dr. Gideon. You remember, he took care of Caleb?"

She nodded and swallowed hard against a rising nausea. For a moment she could have sworn the man was Dooley Kling, all wrapped in furs like that. But Kling wore a beard and was filthy dirty and wrapped himself from head to foot in animal skins. Dr. Gideon had no facial hair but a neat mustache. Only their size was the same.

She took one last glance at the back of the fur-coated giant and let Lincolnshire lead her into the mercantile store. Warmth from the stove hit her flush in the face, but she continued to shiver, thinking of meeting Dooley Kling face-to-face. A man she hated as much as one could hate any human.

Pretending a composure she didn't feel, she languidly poked among the items on display. Her insides continued to quiver as if she suffered from the ague.

Lincolnshire evidently took her strange behavior as long as he could, then, exasperated with her silence, whispered in her ear, "What was that all about, anyway? Do you not remember the doctor at all?" He stared at her as if she were demented, and she attempted a smile.

"Of course I remember him. It was the coat, I suppose. I only saw him...I just...that is, he reminded me of...oh, I don't know. I guess I'm just not used to being around so many people. It's so noisy and dirty here, and from up on the hill it's so pretty."

"Who is Dooley King?" Lincolnshire picked up a thimble and twirled it around on his pinky finger, pale eyes pinning her.

There was no use resisting. "Kling, not King. Dooley Kling. He was Caleb's father." She pointed the statement and her chin at him like an accusation.

He backed off, fast, as if embarrassed for both of them, and became very interested in bolts of cloth.

She had no idea if Rose had told this man anything about her situation, past her need for a job and a home, and she certainly had no intention of doing so.

In comparison to feeding twenty to thirty men, the eleven who had stayed on at the mine for the winter seemed easy, and she found herself with some free time. After that brief and terrifying episode with Dr. Gideon, she began to take walks every afternoon between dinner and cooking the final meal of the day. Wrapped only in a shawl, for the sun warmed daily, she would circle the compound around the mess tent, then stand above the town gazing down and thinking of Dooley Kling. She hadn't been able to get him out of her thoughts since mistaking Dr. Gideon for him.

Behind her, on the mountainside, the fiercely powerful jets of water ground away at the rising terrain, blasting out great chunks of earth and ore. Lincolnshire's use of hydraulic mining, scoffed at when he had the equipment hauled in, was a great success. Even now, with work curtailed for the winter months, the sluices carried hundreds of times the amount of gold an individual miner could ever hope to pan.

As the weeks went by, rushing headlong toward spring, a longing took root in her heart and soul. A longing so profound and melancholy that she found herself unable to resist. Day after day, as the sound of Dooley Kling's monstrous voice haunted her, she thought more and more of those sweet weeks spent with Reed Bannon. Even the worst of them were better than any since. As a child she had longed for love, and now the dark-eyed and gentle Reed Bannon began to walk with her in her dreams. She had no idea what was happening to her, but a birthing of spirit soft and clean as the touch of falling snow began to nourish a faint hope in her breast.

On a day when the ice-blue sky was laced with fingers of gold, she left the huge tent at the Lincolnshire Mines on foot. It was a Sunday afternoon, settling day in Virginia City, the day all the miners went to town with their gold to settle their debts and make their week's purchases. All places of business, including the saloons and hurdy-gurdy houses, were wide open. It wasn't unusual for many of the men to carry their Saturday night carousing on into Sunday without bothering to sleep between.

She waited until Lincolnshire rode out on his favorite shaggy black mare before starting down the muddy road into town. He would have taken her to town had she asked, but she didn't want to answer any questions. And she certainly didn't want him trailing along after her. This was to be a day of discovery and decision, and she needed to do it without help.

As her booted feet sank into the mire left behind by melting ice and snow, she breathed deeply of the smoky, warming air. She thrived in the high altitude, enjoyed its arid embrace, the smell of pine and the sight of jagged precipices. What an exciting wildness of spirit dwelt here. If she could find Reed, they could live high up in those mountains the rest of their lives.

So engrossed in thought was she that the approaching carriage drew up beside her without her noticing.

"Tressie, Tressie, child," cried a familiar voice, bringing her out of her reveries.

To her delight she gazed up into the face of Rose Langue, nested in white fur. How wonderful to have her friend back again. She hoisted herself into the carriage and crawled into the luxurious fur robes, both women laughing and exclaiming over each other.

Rose called out to her driver, "Take us back to the Golden Sun, Enoch."

"Yes'm," he replied, and clicked his tongue at the fine black mare pulling the rig.

"When did you get back?" Tressie asked.

"Late yesterday, and I must confess I'm still exhausted by the trip. I couldn't bear to be away when spring erupted. No sight is quite as glorious as watching these mountains come to life. How have you been, dear?" Rose found Tressie's gloved hands with her own and clasped them. "Maggie told me of your loss. I'm so dreadfully sorry about the child. He was so lovely. I have to confess I cried. Are you recovering?"

Tressie's eyes teared, but she nodded. She did, after all, have to get on with things. All thoughts of wanting to be alone this day vanished. Rose was just the tonic she needed. The older woman's presence would soothe even the saddest of souls, and it was difficult to remain depressed when she was around.

"And now, what is this story I hear about you? Jarrad says you hardly leave that dreadful mess tent. Don't do that, child, don't withdraw from life. You're so young, you must move on. Fall in love, have some fun before it's too late. Goodness knows, there's little enough pleasure. But you know how I feel about taking pleasure where it comes." The sound of Rose's glorious laugh warmed the dark corners of Tressie's mind.

She squeezed her friend's hand. "Oh, Rose, I didn't realize how much I missed you. I haven't realized a lot of things for a long, long time. And then when Caleb died, I guess it all just got wiped out. I don't even know where I've been these last months, and I can't remember anything but sorrow. What am I going to do now? What?"

Rose embraced her, held her head to her shoulders. What a sad life this child had lived so far. How to teach her to enjoy what was left? To take huge bites and savor each and every one as if it were the last, and have absolutely no regrets. She patted Tressie's head. "What do you want to do?"

"If I knew that, I'd do it."

Rose chuckled. "I doubt it. You're too timid, child. Even if you could come up with a plan, you'd wallow it around until you found some reason not to carry through. For once in your life, do something just for the hell of it."

Enoch pulled up the mare. "We here, Miss Rose."

"Yes. Come on, Tressie. Let's go in and have a hot toddy and catch up. I'm anxious to hear all the news since I've been gone."

To Enoch she said, "Don't unhitch the buggy. You'll be taking Miss Tressie back later."

Rose's gay mood was catching, and soon Tressie was chattering away as she followed Rose into the Golden Sun Saloon and up the wide staircase.

Settled on the matching chaise lounges, holding steaming cups of lemon water dashed with honey and whiskey, the two women delighted in their reunion.

"We went to the theater at least once a week," Rose said. "It was such fun. And the new fashions. One must wonder, what with the war dragging on so, how merchants could possibly think of things like feathered hats and fur muffs, but in St. Louis they do. I brought you something that will perk up those sad eyes, child."

Tressie relaxed and sipped at the toddy, feeling its fire all the way to her marrow. This was precisely what she had needed. A giddy, devil-may-care afternoon in which absolutely nothing mattered. "You shouldn't have, but I'm glad you did," she told Rose. "Oh, it's so good to have you back. I've missed you so. Does Mr. Lincolnshire know you're here?"

Rose tipped her glass up and drank lustily. "Yes, indeed. We had our reunion last night. Most of the night, in fact, if you must know. He hasn't changed. Just as randy as ever. I think my absence has done wonders. He couldn't leave me alone."

Tressie flushed and changed the subject. "Why didn't he tell me you were here? I saw him at breakfast."

Rose chuckled. "I asked him not to. I wanted to surprise you by riding out this morning, but you turned the tables on me. What were you doing on foot on that dreadful road?"

"I'm not sure. I just knew that I had to do something today or I would explode. Everything's coming to life, Rose. And I'm fit to burst inside with a need for something, and I don't even know what it is. Yet, when I think like that, thoughts of Caleb and having to bury him intrude. And about the time I get them put back in their place, Reed Bannon crops up. Oh, Rose, why are men such jackasses?"

Rose whooped and set her glass down on the round table between them. "Might as well ask why the moon shines, or the snow falls. That's just the way of things, and the sooner we face it, the better. Who is this Reed Bannon, and what did he do to you? Is he Caleb's father? What's been going on while I've been off having a good time?"

Tressie had never mentioned Reed to Rose. There never seemed to be the appropriate time, and she was ashamed to admit to her brief fling. Rose did think her chaste in her ways. But now she blurted out the whole story, glossing over nothing.

Rose listened raptly, never interrupting till Tressie wound down. "And even right up till he put me on the stage I thought he might come along, but he didn't. He just stood there watching me and Caleb ride away. I know he loved me as much as I loved him. I still do love him, but it does no good at all. He's gone for good, and I still miss him. Oh, Rose, I'm so ashamed for being such a fool."

"Hogwash. Men have a way of fooling women, no doubt, but if you truly love a man, then do what you must to get him and keep him. If you lose…" She shrugged ivory shoulders.

"I suppose. And I guess I've lost this time, Rose. I'm tired of it. I don't care if I ever see another man."

Rose stretched and stood. "Well, sweetie, I wouldn't go that far if I were you. Just keep your mind on straight, that's all. But don't give up on all men. They can be downright enjoyable."

"Is that how you feel about Lincolnshire?"

Rose flushed and touched her bosom lightly with the flat of a hand. "Of course, what else? There's no need in loving the man, now, is there?"

But Tressie no more believed her friend than she believed the end of the world was at hand.

Rose bustled over to a huge trunk sitting on end, open to reveal an array of colorful costumes. She fingered through them, selecting a shimmering cobalt-blue dress that might have been plucked from the spring sky. Yards of material draped softly away from a softly gathered bodice that fastened up the back. Billowy long sleeves and high neckline were trimmed with ribbons and tiny pearls. Tressie gasped in disbelief. She had never seen anything so lovely.

Rose lifted it up under Tressie's chin. "Perfect," she murmured. "Undress. Get out of that dowdy rag."

While Tressie disrobed, Rose spread the dress across the bed and rummaged around until she came up with a corset.

"Everything. Down to the nubbin, girl."

"Rose?" Tressie asked tremulously as she slipped out of her bloomers.

"Yes, sweetheart," Rose said, eying the corset thoughtfully.

"Could I have a bath first?"

"Well, my darling, of course you may. Let me get you a robe and I'll have some water brought. Why am I so thoughtless? I'll bet you've been bundled in long johns all the winter long, haven't you?"

Tressie, who had never gone a day without a bath before coming into this uncivilized country, nodded mutely. "I just grab a quick wash first thing in the morning. A bath would be heaven."

Rose tossed her a lavender robe as luxurious as any she'd ever seen and left the room. Soon buckets of hot water arrived carried by young men who glanced only furtively in Tressie's direction before dumping them into the marvelous tub. Rose didn't return while Tressie lolled up to her neck in fragrant bubbles.

Rubbing the thick cloth over a bar of scented soap, she cleansed her body, using slow, languorous strokes that awakened every fiber of her being. Her skin tingled and she grew warm and flushed. When she finished the wash, she sank down until water lapped her chin and closed her eyes.

Absently, she trailed one finger over her breasts and down past her belly button to the nest of fine reddish hair.

A sleeping desire awakened there, reaching and throbbing with exquisite pain. She touched its swollen head and cried out. Here, after months of stumbling numbly through her days, Tressie Majors found herself astoundingly alive.

Rose returned to discover her young friend lying dreamily in the cooling water. "Let's wash that lovely head of hair, too," she said. "If you're finished, that is."

Tressie agreed she was and Maggie came in with fresh water to help.

"It's grown a lot over the winter," Rose remarked combing out the tangles of curls. They fell past her shoulders. "We'll do it up after you get dressed."

Tressie stood before the looking glass, scarcely able to believe her eyes. The glorious blue cloud of a dress, her hair fastened at the top of her head and cascading down around her face in bouncing curls, the touch of color Rose had applied carefully to her skin. Where had that radiant creature in the mirror come from? She'd thought her dead and gone.

"Oh, Rose. Look at me. Oh, thank you. Thank you." She pirouetted and glanced into the mirror over her shoulder. She took a step or two, then became conscious of the rug under her bare feet. Lifting the dress carefully, she wiggled her toes. "What about these?"

"Oh, slippers, yes, of course." Rose fetched several pair and they were all a little tight. Or perhaps Tressie only thought so because for so long she had worn outsized shapeless footwear. She would grow used to these, she determined, and took a few mincing steps.

"Let's go downstairs, let everyone have a look. What do you say?" Rose enthused.

"Oh, I don't know," Tressie said in a small voice.

Hands planted on her hips, Rose said, "You don't mean to tell me you're not going to let anyone see you after all that hard work. Nonsense."

Grabbing Tressie's hand, she dragged her across the room and to the top of the stairs.

The saloon was crowded with miners, including some Tressie knew from the Lincolnshire Mines. Rose clapped her hands loudly. "Attention, everyone. I present, straight from her debut, Miss Tressie Majors."

Every eye turned her way and she wanted to run back to the room, but Rose wouldn't let her. Instead she urged her, step by careful step, down the long staircase while everyone in the room cheered and shouted and held up dripping mugs of brew. She must be blushing wildly, but there was no stopping Rose.

Just as she put her foot down from the last step, the batwing doors swung open, letting in a tall man who stopped when he caught sight of her. The hanging lamp cast a shadow from the wide brim of his gray hat so that she couldn't make out his features. But when he swept it off and said, "My God in heaven," she nearly fainted.

Her heart slammed against her rib cage so hard she could scarcely breathe. Then she just stood there, arms limp at her sides, as Reed Bannon crossed the room in huge strides and captured her trembling body. She would have fallen had he not wrapped her in a vigorous embrace.

Four

When Reed saw Tressie standing there, all clouded in sky blue, little smudges under her eyes, their green shining like she'd been through hell but was coming back anyway, he nearly whooped with the glory of it. He forgot he couldn't have her love. He just stumbled forward, losing his hat as he wrapped her up in both arms, snugged her tightly just where she belonged, against his thundering heart.

She clung to what she could. Fingers threaded through the shaggy black hair, her head resting against a shoulder as hard as iron, as giving as feathery down. The joy of such a miracle spread through her sweet as honey.

"Reed, it's you. Oh, Reed," she said into the unfamiliar beard.

To cheers from the miners he danced her around the room. In the borrowed slippers, her feet scarcely touched the floor. He smelled of the trail and damp woolens worn too long, but she didn't care. She could only repeat in a somewhat dazed mumble, "You came back, you came back."

"You bet I did, darlin'. Oh, Lord, you're lovely as spring. Do you know how much I've missed you?" He plopped her down on the far end of the bar and backed away a step to gaze with awe, never breaking contact: spanning her waist, grasping her hands, touching fingertips to the flushed skin of her face.

A wave of anger swept over her. "Where have you been? Where did you go?"

Drawing her close, he kissed her tightened lips to another wave of applause and shouting. At last he realized he was performing for an audience and set her down. He captured her hand and ignored the frown creasing her forehead.

"Go? Where did I go? Away from you, and I'll always be sorry for that. Come on." He tugged her toward the dance floor, where two or three couples swayed in the dimness.

But she couldn't stem the fury growing inside. Born of grief and loneliness and despair, it spewed out at him in a bitter tirade. "No. I don't work here, Reed, and I'm not at your beck and call. You want a whore, buy a ticket and I'll fetch one of the girls."

Justly deserved, those words. They were payment for deserting her, for making her go through Caleb's death alone, for taking back his love when she needed it the most. He had to be punished; he couldn't just return like this free of blame, expecting her to take up where they'd left off. Nothing was the same, nor would it ever be. And he had to realize that before they could seek a way to go on.

To his total dismay, she whirled and, lifting the billowing blue skirts, raced up the stairs. She flew past Rose, who was rooted in place near the banister.

The saloon owner let her go, studied the tall dark man. Eyes cloudy with pain, he extended one arm and seemed to freeze that way. Rose went to him. Taking his limp and unresisting hand, she led him to the bar and bought him a beer. She was afraid that if he left now, Tressie would never forgive him or herself. Rose intended to lend a gentle hand, guide circumstances just a bit in the direction she thought they should go.

"My name is Rose Langue, and I own this place. And who might you be?" By now she had guessed his identity, but he needed to tell it.

In a voice hoarse with surprise, he said his name. After lifting the glass to take a hefty swallow, he shook his head as if perplexed. "Thank you."

"She'll be all right," Rose said.

He shifted a quick look around, taking in the scantily dressed women lounging around the dance floor. "Quite a place," he remarked, then cleared his throat. "She doesn't—"

"Lord, no. Not her." Rose laughed robustly. "Not that I didn't try, mind you. No, she's been cooking up at the Lincolnshire Mines."

"Then, what?" He gestured into space as if he could bring back the earlier scene with all its poignancy.

"We're friends. She's had a rough time, what with the baby dying and all. I—"

The woman might as well have struck him physically with such news. He would have staggered had he not been leaning on the bar. "Caleb? He died? Oh, dear God. What happened?"

Rose squeezed at the beer mug with both hands and motioned toward his empty glass. He shook his head, feeling sick. "I don't understand. What happened?"

"Get her to tell you," Rose said. "She needs to talk about it with someone who cares." She paused and pointed a shrewd look at him. "You do care?"

"Hell, yes, I care. I've been looking for her since I realized what a mistake I made sending her off like I did. If it wasn't for…well, for my own stupidity, I—"

"Did you know her papa?"

Reed shook his head vigorously. "No. And I hope to God I never do, the bastard. Leaving his family out in the middle of nowhere to starve to death. Wonder she didn't die out there, too, and him not even caring enough to come back."

Rose pursed her lips. "Maybe he couldn't. Did you ever think that maybe he's the one who died?"

He snapped his head around. "No, no. I never once thought that. What I did think was that she'd ruin her life looking for vengeance. She loves the scoundrel, and that's double trouble. She deserves better than me—And I... I ain't much better."

"And so you took the coward's way out. Deserted her just like he did."

His own thoughts, thrown back at him so precisely, fed Reed's self-contempt so that he was forced to defend himself against this strange woman's judgment.

"Now, you wait a doggone minute." Reed half turned to face Rose, and when he did he saw Tressie, standing at the top of the stairs, stiff as a ramrod, looking down at him.

He drew a ragged breath and Rose glanced over her shoulder. She shoved at him. "Go on to her. Go upstairs and shut yourselves up in my room and get this hashed out. If you don't, you'll both always be sorry."

Tressie watched Reed cross the room in long strides, his intent stare ever on her. Tears leaked from the corners of her eyes, but she ignored them. His cave-dark gaze caught hers, sending a shimmer of desire through her.

He came up the steps, reaching one hand out to her before he reached the top. She gave him her trembling fingers and he lifted them to his mouth. The moist warmth of his tongue sent a surge of elation straight to her heart and she smiled through her tears.

"Oh, dear Tressie. My sweet darlin' Tressie." He folded her into his arms. "I'm so sorry. I never meant to hurt you, I only wanted what was best, I truly did."

"Shh, shh, it's okay, Reed. I know, I know. It was just so awful and dark without you."

The terrible dread lifted from his mind and heart, and he dared to hope. "Rose said to use her room. Where—"

"This way." She pulled him through the door, backing up against it to shut out the world.

At the sound of the latch, both turned suddenly shy. Alone, shut away from prying eyes, they weren't sure what might happen next.

She gestured toward one of the chaise lounges. "Sit down. Tell me where you've been, what you've been doing."

He rubbed both hands down the front of his shirt, disrupting clouds of dust. How trail-weary he looked and felt. Mud covered his boots, had splashed up the legs of pants tucked into their tops. He looked at the brocaded fabric of the lounge. "I can't. Look at me."

She did, seeing a broad-shouldered, well-muscled man who could use a bath. Otherwise he was the finest sight she'd beheld in recent memory. "I see you, Reed. Come over here to me."

He did, but sank to the floor and let her draw his head into her lap. With caring fingers she traced the line of his strong whiskered jaw, flitted her touch over his lips, and then brushed the hair off his forehead. He closed his eyes and sighed.

"Would you like a hot bath?" she whispered in his ear.

Reed couldn't help laughing. How like her. "Oh, darlin', you and your baths. It would be great. I feel like I've got half the territory hanging on my britches. But I'm too tired and happy to move."

"Oh, you won't have to move much. Just lift your head so I can go see to the hot water. You stay here and rest." She slid from under his weight and patted the chaise. "Put it there, and I'll be right back."

He grabbed at her hand. 'Tressie?"

She turned sparkling summery-green eyes on him, waited. "Don't go very far. I don't want to lose you again."

"I won't," she said, then kissed the tips of two of her fingers and touched them to his lips. "Be right back."

He was half asleep when the buckets of hot water began to arrive. He watched in amazement as the steaming tub grew rich with bubbles and deep with water. Tressie followed the bearer of the last two buckets. She carried large towels, a washcloth, and a fresh bar of plain white soap.

Kicking the door shut, she put her load down on a chair near the tub and came to him, fingers going to work on the buttons of his shirt. 'You still dressed?"

When her fingers reached his waist and pulled the shirt from his pants, he took her wrists in his gentle grasp.

"You'd better let me finish that, or we'll never get me in the tub. I swear, woman, I've missed the hell out of you."

He caught her lips to his, tasting, savoring. Though their bodies didn't touch, she just knew her heart would explode right out of her chest.

With reluctance she eased back, said into his mouth, "The water is getting cold."

He nodded. There would be time for everything now.

He crawled to his feet, shucked out of the britches and underclothing, and walked naked to the tub. With a grateful sigh, he climbed in, lowering himself delicately, for the water was still hot. When the bubbles sloshed around his ears, he let out another long-drawn breath. "Oh, that's fine. Real fine."

"Rest awhile," she advised. "From the looks of you, it'll take a good soak to get all that grime off. What you been doing, wrestling buffalo?"

The time would come, Reed knew, when he would have to tell her about the Indian massacre. How he felt that he'd been nothing but a coward, that he should have been able to save his companions. Most men would have been braver, would have figured out something to do before the affair got totally out of hand. But just now, all he wanted was to luxuriate in her company, touch her, get his fill of her exquisite beauty. To have found her again was unbelievable.

He splashed water over his face and scrubbed at the itchy

beard. Leaning back, he closed his eyes. He hadn't felt this good in months. Not since the last time he'd shared a bath with Tressie.

She was content to remain on the chaise lounge and watch him for a long time. All signs of exhaustion drained from his features as he relaxed in the bath. There was something different about him, but she couldn't put her finger on it. A sadness or haunting about the eyes. Other than that he looked much as he had when they parted, except for the beard.

After a while she couldn't stand the room being between them and went to sit in the chair near the tub, holding the towels in her lap.

He fluttered his long lashes open to gaze at her. "Come here," he whispered. A smoky, sensual tone that sent shudders through her.

She glanced down at the lovely blue dress, then began to undo the buttons with trembling fingers.

When she had reached as far as she could both up and down the back, he said, "Here, I'll do those."

She let him, then crossed the room to skin from the dress and petticoats, spreading them out flat on the bed. She was taking her time because she wanted him so badly and that felt so good. Finally, down to a corset and pantaloons, she returned to him. He worked at the lacing, at last releasing her from the tight bonds. Her gasp of relief brought nervous laughter to them both.

Embarrassed now, as if she'd never stood naked before him, she said shyly, "I'm not sure I'm made for such as that."

"Women will wear anything," he remarked, and turned her around to gaze with delight.

Smooth creamy skin, round firm breasts, rosy nipples. So familiar, so exquisite. Tongue caught between his lips, he hooked his thumbs in her bloomers and eased them down as far as he could reach.

Struck by the delicate loveliness of her young body, he could scarcely speak, and scooted up straight in the tub to make room. "Get in here with me, can you?"

She only hesitated a moment. Her flesh throbbed with a need for him, the renewed desire a living, breathing thing. She imagined his rigid maleness made slick by the hot soapy water, thought of how it would feel slipping deep inside her aching body. Before this very moment Tressie had never realized how much of her suffering had been tied up with missing this man.

She wanted never to let him free again. Wanted to touch him, to love him, to make him cry out with passion and desire and need. Wanted to rid herself forever of the pain of not having him.

In a hurry, she wrenched off the shoes and stockings and posed that way briefly, giving him a good look. His tongue rolled out and moistened his lips. She touched it with the tips of her fingers, his hand rippled across the flesh of her belly. From deep down inside her came a moan of desire and need that hurt in its intensity.

When she lifted one leg to climb in the tub, he laid his palm on the inside of her thigh and brushed at the bristle of pubic hair with one thumb tip. Her heart thundered and she bit at her lip, overcome by ecstasy. His thumb explored some more and she eased into the tub, holding his hand in place with the pressure of both thighs.

Under the bubbles she caressed his legs, working upward until she had him firmly in hand.

He growled and cupped her breast gently, kneading the nipple in a languorous motion. Bending forward, he lapped the rosebud into his mouth. He would never let her go again. Not for anyone, not for any reason.

A yearning grew within his soul, his mind, his body, to overpower the doubts he had about himself. By giving herself to him she proved her love, and he embraced that gift, hoping to God he could live up to the expectations that were bound to come with it. A blinding passion temporarily drowned the fears lurking just beyond his need for this exquisite woman and he reached out.

Tressie slid forward, guided him into her, and held his mouth at her breast a moment longer. His arms tightened; he moaned, then cried out. Together they rocked in pure ecstasy that shut out the room, sent them soaring into a place of pure bliss.

"This must be the way it feels to be born," she murmured just before the world went from a shadowy black to a pearlescent white that consumed her in its purity.

For long moments afterward, he felt unsure of where he was. Did he even want to return from that intense and all-encompassing place? Then he began to stir, clinging to her, finally rewrapping his arms, this time around her shoulders because she was slick with soap and he couldn't seem to hang on. Her breath tickled at his ear and he turned his head so that their lips met.

Slipping both hands into her hair, he loosened what pins were left there and fingered its fiery tresses free. "You are the most lovely thing in this world."

"Thing? Thing?" she breathed back.

"Yes. Yes. Of all the things: mountains, rivers, plains, and oceans, women, children, clouds, sky. All things."

"Oh, I love you. What are we going to do? It's still the same, isn't it?"

"No. I won't let it be," he said almost harshly, then grinned into her face. "Look at you. All wet and bedraggled, like a newborn calf."

He wanted only to keep her from thinking those thoughts, and he would do whatever it took.

"A newborn calf? Well, sir, that does it." She wanted to go along with this all the way. She had no desire to go back into that blank nothingness of her existence up to this moment.

"It's time I scrubbed your ears. There's a crop of grass sprouting in there. And this hair, all over you. Just look at that."

She went to work on him, using the washcloth and the bar of white soap. Lathering the thick black hair, she mounded up the suds into peaks that turned him into a mystical being with glistening eyes. He grimaced, made a face that caused her to howl in delight. She soaped up the beard and giggled when he sputtered flecks of foam.

"Lift your arm, you," she said, still chuckling. She washed in mock severity, first one arm, then the other. Then came his chest, and the lower she went, the more intent became their concentration.

"O-ho, what's this?" she finally asked. "You ought to be ashamed of yourself, sir. Some modicum of control would be called for in this situation."

"In this situation, madam, there can be no modicum of control," he retorted. "If you want this bath finished, I suggest you start at the other end and work your way up. Then when you reach—uh—the critical point once again, I'll be clean and we can…well ... we can take care of this rising problem."

"An animal, that's all you are," she scolded, and pivoted, straddling his legs so her back was to him.

It took a while to wash his toes because he claimed to be ticklish, causing quite a wrestling match that sloshed water everywhere. They reached the critical point some time later, and the water grew cold around them before they finally slaked the desire each had for the other.

Crawling from the tub, they moved to the bed. There, wrapped in generous towels, they lay in each other's arms.

"Rose may want her room back sometime soon," he said while twining a curl of her hair around his finger.

"Um-hum, I suppose."

"Where do you live?" he asked.

"Up at the mine, in the back of the mess tent, behind the cookstove."

"Oh, Tressie, my dear sweet girl. I'm so sorry." Tears tickled at his throat and he swallowed their burning saltiness.

"It's okay. It's not so bad. It's warm and I have plenty to eat and a place to sleep. But we couldn't both—"

"What can we both do? We can't take advantage of Rose's good graces much longer. And I don't have any gold dust."

Tressie grinned and raised to one elbow. "I do."

"What? You have gold dust? Been out panning, my child?" he asked *sotto voce.*

"No, but I get paid in gold for cooking up at the mine, and other than a few clothes, I haven't needed much. It's hidden in my mattress."

"Oh, Tressie. Some things never do change. First you give me a bath before bed, now you tell me you still keep your poke in the mattress."

"Well, it's as good a place as any, I guess…Wait a minute, how did you know I kept it there before? I never told you, and you were gone before I took it out. That reminds me, you louse. It's time you told me what you've been up to."

"I will, darlin', I will. Just as soon as we get out of here. What did you have in mind?"

She shrugged and sat up, holding the towel over her breasts. "A hotel, I guess."

"And let you pay for it? How low can a man sink?"

"Depends entirely on how badly he wants what he wants," she shot back smartly.

"You should be ashamed of yourself, trying to buy my favors with a few ounces of gold."

She grinned and tugged at a hank of his shining and damp black hair. "I just can't resist a thing of such beauty."

Just as he lunged for her and she darted away, dropping the towel at her feet, a knock sounded on the door.

"It's Rose," came the woman's lilting voice. "Come to claim what's mine. Are you decent?"

"Not so you would notice," he shouted, and Tressie threw her wadded towel at him.

"Give us a few minutes, Rose," she said, and shook a finger at him. He laughed and rolled off the bed.

They dressed amid the confusion of trying to help each other and Reed's bemoaning putting his dirty clothes back on.

"You could send them out to the Chinese laundry and we could parade through the saloon with you wrapped in a towel," Tressie suggested as she urged him to button up her dress, the plain muslin one she'd arrived in, not the blue one Rose had bought her in St. Louis.

"What about that…that other thing—you know." He cupped his hands under her breasts and shoved them up.

"That's just for special occasions. Only women who have little to do would go around strapped into one of those things."

He tweaked her breasts before going back to his buttoning job. "Special occasions, huh?

"Oh, well, of course, this isn't one of those. And just what is it you expect to get done? Other than just walk from here to that hotel, where you'll be coming right out of this again?"

He took her upper arms in both hands and turned her around to face him. Her hair hung loose to her shoulders, the damp curls fringing her wide eyes and framing the delicate features.

"Oh, Lordy, how did I let you get away?" he asked, and kissed the tip of her nose.

"Put on your boots and let's give Rose back her room."

She picked up the scattered towels and straightened the bed coverlet and hung the blue dress in Rose's armoire. It would keep there very well.

While Reed shoved his feet into the high-top muddy boots, Tressie twisted her hair into a knot and pinned it securely. Immediately tiny ringlets escaped and she poohed at herself.

"Looks fine to me," he said with a chuckle.

"Well, look what poor judgment you have."

He regarded her somberly. "I guess you're right there."

"Oh, I was only teasing."

He knew that, but was thinking of the massacre at the stage station, something she couldn't possibly know about.

"I know," he said. "I'm starved. Do you suppose that gold dust will spread far enough to feed us?"

"How about some venison stew? We have to go back up to the mine, and I left some on the stove."

"Sounds fine to me."

That night in the hotel room she told him about Caleb's death, reluctantly speaking of it for the first time. She glossed over her reaction, other than to tell him she thought she might die of grief for ever so long.

"And you kept your job?"

"Oh, yes. Jarrad Lincolnshire has been very good to me. That's not to say he's good to everyone, though. He treats Rose disgracefully, and she lets him. Sometimes I think the blindness we women suffer when it comes to love is our worst curse."

"No worse than ours, my love. Perhaps he, too, is blinded in a way that prevents him from treating her properly."

"Don't you dare make excuses for a man you don't even know."

"It's not excusing him. It's just I'm saying sometimes behavior has reasons behind it that make perfect sense, if only we knew them."

"Well, he's cheating her. Married and cleaving to his wife while using Rose's feelings for him. Why doesn't he just pay someone he doesn't know if he must satisfy his lust?"

"Yes, indeed. That is cheating her, but perhaps she's willing to take whatever she can get."

She wiggled around and lay staring up into the darkness for a moment. "We're no longer talking about Jarrad and Rose, are we?"

"It's okay, darlin'. No one held a gun to my head. I ran because I was afraid of my feelings for you. Ran more than once, as I recall."

"And I wouldn't let you go. But, you see, that was different. I needed you to rescue me from—"

He hushed her with a kiss, beginning on her bare shoulder and moving over her neck to her lips. It was too dark in the room to see each other, but she could make out the glitter in his eyes, like sparks of life in a dead place.

Could she abandon her search? Give up the one thing that had kept her going when everything crashed down around her: her rueful need to see Papa suffer as much as she and Mama had during those long months alone on the plains in that remote soddy? Cut off from the world, abandoned by the one who had pledged to care for them. Could she then take up with a man who might well do the same thing to her? A man who already had left her once.

She lay stiffly beside him. Maybe it was possible he was right, and the reasons for behavior ought to soften the consequences.

"What if I stopped looking for him? Then what?"

He held his breath. Dear God, he didn't dare make yet another promise he might not keep. This wasn't fair to either of them, and yet he loved her, thought she loved him.

She heard the hesitation, even though he spoke almost immediately, huskily, "Can you?"

"I can try."

"Only try? Tressie, hate eats you up. I know, believe me. If you keep after your pa, keep looking for him in every face you see, keep dreaming of revenge for what he did, you'll never be happy, we'll never be happy. I've run most of my life, and I'm afraid I can't give you what you want, either. I don't know the answer, I don't, except you've got to stop hating your papa. Think of something else to do with your life."

She waited a long, long time before answering, and there were tears in her voice when she did. "I want to be married to the man I love. Have his children. But not until I find Papa and make him pay for what he did. He the same as killed Mama, and he didn't care one whit about me or the baby, either. Do you know what that's like? To know someone you love dearly doesn't even care what happens to you?

"And then you go off and Caleb dies...oh, I'm so confused, so frightened. Please understand. If our love is true, it will last through this. If you can't help me find him, well, then you just don't love me enough, that's all. And I don't want to find that out after we're married and have children.

"Please, I have to find Papa. Damn his soul to hell."

"Ah, Tressie, love, you don't mean that. Don't even say it. You have to forgive him. Please forgive him."

It suddenly became very important to him that she let go of her hate of her papa. He could see it standing between their love like a great bank of storm clouds, hissing and spitting at any move they might make to be happy. He would follow her anywhere, he knew, but his prayer would be not that they find her pa, but that she forgive him.

Dear God, if Tressie couldn't forgive her own father, what made him think she ever could overlook the awful things he himself had done?

He held her tightly, felt the heat of her tears, and came close to joining her in the sobbing.

At last he fell into a deep and troubled sleep, eventually walking a familiar trail that led him through bloody snow to the door of a cabin. It all came back. The smell of blood and death, the sight of the helpless slain, the sound of the woman's scream, growing in intensity until he could dwell there no more. With a shout he lunged bolt upright in the bed. His breath came in jagged gasps and he was covered with sweat.

She touched the hunched back, kneaded the knotted muscles, crept around until she could hold him in her arms.

"Oh, God help me," he said, and grabbed on to her.

"Shh, shh, it's all right. It was only a dream. I'm here, you're here." She rocked him until he stopped shaking, then lowered him back onto the pillow.

Somehow they would have to get through this together. She would not give him up again, but neither would she stop looking for Papa. There simply had to be a way.

Five

Jarrad Lincolnshire eyed Tressie with regret. "We'll miss you, girl. Are you sure this is what you want?"

He aimed a stern look toward Reed Bannon, who stood a few paces away, hat in both hands. His face appeared younger without the beard, the mouth more defined and stubborn. She was glad he had shaved.

Reed scowled and returned Lincolnshire's glare. The two men hadn't hit it off at all, and Tressie was secretly glad. After Reed's making excuses for a man he didn't even know, it served him right to find he disliked that man. Still, despite the relationship between the Englishman and her best friend Rose, she herself couldn't feel anything but grateful to him.

"What will you do?" Lincolnshire asked.

"We're heading up Bannack way. Maybe do some prospecting," Reed injected gruffly.

"Taking her with you? That's no life for a woman. Gold camps are barbaric, unsanitary hellholes," Lincolnshire said. "Let her remain here while you get this out of your system."

He didn't wait for Reed to reply, but turned to Tressie. "Be reasonable, child. Don't let your heart rule your head. He'll work you to death."

Tressie was amazed at Lincolnshire's reaction. She knew he

was fond of her, but this was totally out of reason. He was acting more like her father than an employer and friend.

Touching his arm, she pleaded, "You don't understand. This is what I want. I need to get away from here. We'll be okay. He will take care of me, I promise you."

"Tressie, come on," Reed urged. His face was blotched dark with anger, yet he held back from voicing it. Perhaps in deference to her feelings for this man and what he had done for her and Caleb. Still she had to wonder if he ever cared about a thing enough to explode. If he did, she'd never seen it.

She remembered how sometimes Papa would go into a blue rage, face turning red, fists clenching. On a few occasions he'd actually thrown things. Once he'd scared her half to death by shaking Mama quite roughly when she'd disagreed with him about something. What, she could no longer even remember. Men's anger was generally a frightening thing to see, for they often took it out on their woman. Even so she loved her father, and his few lapses hadn't changed that. But she didn't want to keep remembering things about that life anymore. There was no purpose; it was gone for good, thanks to Papa. Would she never forgive him?

Lincolnshire jerked her back to the present with stern words. "And what about the funeral?"

Tressie clasped both fists tightly against her mouth. She had blotted that from her mind as surely as if Caleb had never existed. Being with Reed had renewed in her a happiness she didn't want to lose. Mention of the funeral yanked her back to a sorrowful reality. "Oh, oh. I never thought…when? When are they going to do it?"

"This coming Saturday: Everyone will be there."

Tressie nodded. "We'll stay for that." She didn't look to Reed for confirmation. There was no question in her own mind.

"Of course we will," Reed echoed. "Until then, Tressie will be staying at the hotel, that is if you can get along without her."

"Oh, but—" Tressie began.

Without giving her time to finish, Lincolnshire whirled and left the tent. His boots squished in the mud as he walked away.

"I could have helped out till he found someone," Tressie said. "No need," Reed replied. "It's best this way, don't you think?" He was probably right, so she didn't argue further.

Late that Friday afternoon, upstairs at the Golden Sun, Rose told Tressie that Maggie had a dress she could wear to the funeral.

Tressie thought it puzzling that Maggie would be the one who could come up with a suitable outfit, but Rose was too busy keeping peace at the Golden Sun to explain. In fact, Maggie was in great demand on the dance floor and it was a while before she came upstairs to talk to Tressie.

The dress she produced was black with a high neck and long sleeves. The girl offered it with tears in her eyes and Tressie mistakenly thought she regretted offering it.

"Oh, no," Maggie replied when asked. "It just brings back bad memories."

Tressie took the dress. "Bad memories. It's so beautiful, but so, well, not you."

"It belonged to my mother. My parents came west with Brigham Young. That was in 1847....I was three. My father and his three wives died. The older children were given out to other families, all except me. I was sick and, they thought, dying. One of the elders left me and my mother's belongings out on the trail with a letter explaining what he had done and why." Maggie paused and touched the dress with trembling fingers.

"Heavens, Maggie. What a terrible thing. What happened? I mean, how did you get here?" Tressie decided there must be nearly as many tragic stories as there were women in the West.

"Little girls are prized by some," Maggie said with a bitter twist to her mouth. "We are never too young, I think, to pleasure some men."

"Oh, Maggie." Tressie put her arm around her friend.

"It's okay. I killed the bastard," Maggie spat. "Just as soon as I was old enough, I waited till he went to sleep after having his way and I shot him in the ear with his own gun."

The two embraced for a moment, but Maggie shed no tears. Tressie felt the despair in the girl's thin body, and thought she understood more about Maggie's desire to care for Caleb when he was sick. Abandoned herself at a young age, she must have felt a certain compassion for the suffering of all children.

"What happened then?" she whispered.

"I was fourteen. I managed to get a ride with a family heading for California. But before we could cross the mountains, the woman caught me and her man out in the woods and run me off. Called me a whore." Maggie pushed away, sighed, and gave Tressie a crooked grin. "And so, since that was what I was, I decided to make the most of it. So here I am." She spread her arms wide. "Oh, shoot. Everyone has a sad story, don't they? Let's see if that dress fits. You need to look your best for the funeral."

Maggie didn't appear at the burying, having given Tressie the only suitable dress she owned. Spring had busted wide open, and the warm weather saw the town filled nearly to bursting with strangers. They, as well as those whose faces were familiar, all attended the mass funeral. After all, such occurrences were social events on the frontier where everyone welcomed any chance to come together.

Tressie stood near Caleb's open grave. Reed held her right arm firmly, Jarrad tucked into her left with Rose next to him. Everyone stood ankle-deep in mud.

Dr. Gideon preached the sermon. It turned out he was a preacher as well as a medical doctor. Holding his stovepipe hat upside down, Bible open across it, the large man began in a melodious voice that carried over the heads of the crowd like the great roar of an avalanche.

As he intoned the service, Tressie steeled herself. A piece of her heart was going in that grave with Caleb. She couldn't help but remember another grave on a windy plain, and prayed this would be the last time she would have to endure such a painful loss. Reed's steadying touch was all that kept her from falling apart. It was almost like losing Caleb again, watching that tiny coffin lowered into the ground along with the others, as one by one the departed of that past harsh winter found their final resting place in Virginia City's cemetery.

Reed eased an arm around her when she sagged against him. Of all the hardships a woman endures, losing a child must be the toughest. And at eighteen she had already seen too much death. Though this child was not born to her, he couldn't help but think that caring for Caleb so deeply had made him her very own. God, how he regretted not having been here to help when she needed him.

His gaze shifted toward the preacher, a mountain of a man who reminded him of Dooley Kling. It was the size more than anything, but the voice struck a chord, too. Reed hadn't wasted much thought on Kling since the man had taken off and deserted his own baby back in the mountains. More important things had intruded.

He did, however, still resent Kling's theft of the soft leather pouch he had carried with him since leaving his mother's people. It was all he had left of his past. Why had the man taken such a valueless thing?

Tressie buried her face in his chest, shoulders quivering as she cried, and he turned his attention back to her. Damn, he hated her having to suffer.

As the crowds drifted away, their voices carried off by a brisk chill wind, Jarrad Lincolnshire and Rose Langue lingered, loath to say good-bye to the young woman they'd grown so fond of.

Ignoring Reed, who remained at Tressie's side, Lincolnshire

said, "I fear for you, dear child. There's no telling what will happen to you, out there amongst all those heathens."

Before she could defend their decision, Reed said, "It'll be all right. We'll do just fine. I'm going to make a place for her." He turned his dark gaze to Rose. "I promise I won't let anything happen to her. And we'll come back and visit sometime."

Rose cocked her head and studied the tall, dark-skinned man. "You're going to try to find Evan Majors, aren't you? That's what you're really up to, a fool's errand."

Tressie glanced quickly at Reed. They had neither spoken of Papa again, as if in keeping quiet both could make his ghostly presence go away. She knew he was right about her need to punish Papa. His silence now spoke volumes. He would be there even though he didn't agree.

"I just can't stop looking for him yet. It's not his idea, don't blame him. I have to know why Papa left, don't you see? I have to find out what made him do that to us, so I can make sure it never happens to me. Oh, Rose, please understand."

The muscles of the arm Reed held around her tightened. "Come on, we have to be getting started," he said softly.

Tressie went along, picking her way through the mud. Rose and Lincolnshire followed. In her most secret self, Rose envied Tressie the love of a man like Reed Bannon. Jarrad Lincolnshire had announced that he would return to London soon to visit with his family. If things worked out, his wife and daughters would return to this new Montana Territory with him. He would build them a home. A castle, he said.

And what will I have? Rose had wanted to ask, but she hadn't. After all, she had expected nothing, why should she now complain? There were other men. She wiped at hot tears that flowed without warning down her cheeks.

As always, she would survive. She wondered how much longer that would be enough.

That night in the hotel room, Reed, in the midst of planning their departure, asked Tressie, "That man, that Gideon. Do you know him well? I can't get him out of my mind."

"I've often felt the same. He took care of Caleb, but I didn't know he was a preacher, too. Isn't that strange?"

"More than strange. He reminds me of Dooley Kling. How long has he been in Virginia City?"

"He arrived after I did, I'm not sure exactly when, though. But you know, he reminds me of Dooley Kling, too, except—"

Reed glanced up from the list he'd worked steadily on all evening. The lamplight brought out the rich coppery tones in Tressie's hair and softened the grief on her features. In her white nightdress, gathered around her neck with a delicate blue ribbon, she was so lovely it made his heart ache. And made him not pay enough attention to what she had just said—not at that moment, anyway.

"They're right, you know," he murmured, and chewed on the end of his pencil.

"About what?"

"You'll be in great danger out there with all those miners so starved for female company."

"I'll not wait here while you look for Papa. I won't be alone anymore." The idea he might leave her was terrifying.

"I won't leave you. I just thought…"

"You don't even know what he looks like."

"It's too hard a life, Tressie. This prospecting. Who said anything about your father?" He almost choked on the words.

She began to cry, making no sound at it, but turning loose a great flood of tears.

"Aw, hell, darlin'. You know I can't stand that." He unwound himself from his chair, put down the pencil, and went to the bed where she sat. When he got there she threw herself at him, hanging on and sobbing.

"If you leave me again, I'll die," she wailed. It was all too much. Her world spiraled away from her. She would promise anything, do anything, to go with him.

He held her close, big hands patting clumsily at the loose braid she'd put in her hair. He could not hurt her more than she'd already been hurt. "It's okay. I won't leave you. We'll go together, and we'll find him or what happened to him. And when we do…well, then…" He didn't know what else to say because he still wasn't completely sure of her love for him.

But she was, and she finished for him. "Then we can be free to start over."

In silence he nodded. All he knew for certain was that he could not watch her ride out on her search alone. She would do that, despite anything he could say. And so he had little choice but to go with her. Worrying about her out there alone on the trail among all those rough miners and whoever else might be at large was much worse than worrying about a Union soldier one day running him down, or some of Quantrill's men stringing him up.

From outside the hotel room, gunshots and shouts erupted. "What in the hell is that?" Reed said.

They rose to go to the window. Down in the muddy street, men in ever-growing numbers rode horses and shouted and fired off their weapons. About that time, there was a huge commotion out in the hallway, and Reed, followed closely by Tressie, raced to open the door.

"What the thunderation is going on?" he asked a bewhiskered man scurrying along, fastening his pants in haste.

"The war, man. It's the war. They say it's over. Lee surrendered today. Not sure where, but they say the war's over."

Reed staggered backward, pushing the door shut. So it was over at last. Much as he hated the killing and the futility, the raping, burning, and looting, he had dreaded this day. For now would come the most devastating of wars. Union soldiers would cover up the West like a gigantic and hungry ocean, and the Indians, who up to now had managed to hold their own, would be wiped from the face of the earth. How tragic there wasn't room for both the red man and the white in this great country. But he sensed the massacres coming and knew he had no choice but to come down on the white man's side. Though he felt a deep affinity for his mother's people, he truly did not belong with them. Not in body or in spirit.

"Reed, are you all right? Isn't it wonderful? Now all those boys can go home." she tugged at his shirtsleeve. "What is it? You're pale as a sheet."

"Nothing," he said softly. "I'm okay." Taking both her hands in his, he raised them to his lips and gazed intently into her shining, summer-grass eyes. "I was just remembering something I hadn't thought of in a while. But it's okay, that's in the past. We have to look to the future now, for sure. There'll be legions of folks moving west as soon as they get over this war. We haven't seen anything out here compared to what it will be. We need to be on our way, find what it is we want."

He led her back to the bed. "Here, sit. I just thought of something. Back when I was working for Dacota, I heard about this stage driver—tough old coot, as I recall—who died. And guess what?"

Tressie was confused. Why was he talking about some old stage driver dying?

"He was a she. They didn't even know it till the undertaker went to, well, you know...."

She turned disbelieving eyes on him. "And so?"

"And so, that's what we'll do. We'll cut your hair, though God knows I hate to see those gorgeous curls shorn, dress you up like a boy. We'll get by with it, and the men won't bother you. What do you think? It's perfect."

Tressie gaped at his ear-to-ear grin. "A–a boy?"

"Yes, don't you see? You can be my little brother."

"Are you serious? You can't be. I'd never get away with it."

"Sure you would. Who would pay that much attention anyway? No one truly looks at anyone. How do you think that old coot got away with passing for a man...all her life, Tressie? We'll just be doing it for a few months, until we make our way through all the gold strike towns. Once we find your pa, then you can become my girl again. It'll work—you'll see."

His excitement was catching, and she rose to look at herself in the wavey mirror above the washstand. "Too bad I can't grow whiskers," she joked after a moment's perusal.

He came up behind her and locked his arms around her waist. "Well, don't get too carried away. I'm not sure how I'd feel kissing someone with whiskers."

She turned in his arms and rubbed up against his chest. "I don't see why; it doesn't bother me in the least," she murmured, and raised her mouth to his.

The next morning she went to see Rose while he used her gold to outfit them for their journey. She promised to meet him at the mercantile in time to buy some clothing suitable for herself. "I just want to tell her goodbye."

The town was still in an uproar over the news of the war's ending. Some men, grateful for any excuse to celebrate, had spent the night in one of the several saloons, gambling, drinking and whoring. It had been an all-night party that hadn't ceased yet, but was losing momentum as the revelers grew too drunk to walk.

Weary horses, tied to hitching rails for many hours, had left piles of manure along the edges of the main street of town. The stink was overpowering.

In the Golden Sun, several girls held up exhausted miners to shuffle around the dance floor.

Rose and her bartender, helped out by her livery man,

Enoch, were busy dragging unconscious patrons out onto the boardwalk in order to clean up the place.

"Isn't this something?" The blonde saloon owner laughed. "I haven't had so much business in one night since the Alder Gulch gold strike. Maybe we ought to have the end of wars more often." Allowing Enoch and the bartender to finish up, Rose took Tressie's arm and they went upstairs together.

"I can't stay but a moment. I just came to say goodbye." "So you're going anyway?"

"Surely you never thought I wouldn't. I love him, Rose. He's gentle and kind. Why would I not go with him? Besides, he came up with a great idea, one that should make you happy."

Rose hugged her friend. "It'll take a humdinger to make me happy with you going out there in that wilderness, child."

"Don't worry about me. He's got a plan that will keep me as safe as any man in the camps. I'm going to cut all my hair off and go dressed as a boy. I'll be his younger brother."

Rose stared in dismay. "That's the craziest thing I ever heard. You'll no more resemble a man than I would, if for different reasons. A young boy would be no safer, I'd wager, than a young girl."

"Of course I would. With Reed, no one will even look twice at a younger companion who looks like a boy. It's a wonderful idea," Tressie finished, but tears glistened in her eyes. "Please wish me well, Rose. I don't think I can stand leaving with you feeling like this."

"Oh, child," Rose said with a sigh. "It's just that I worry so about you. Of course I wish you well. I just don't understand why you and he don't homestead some land and forget all this other nonsense. You don't have to traipse all over gold country looking for that no-good polecat. Just let it be, is what I say."

"I can't, Rose. My mama died and Evan Majors, my papa, well, I won't leave it at that. He'll learn what he did, face me and tell me why, or I'll die trying. Reed says I'm wrong, but he's going with me anyway. He says—"

"Oh, he says foot," Rose said, and paced across the floor. "If that's not just like a man. Damn their hides anyway. I don't understand why they just can't accept what we offer without all this man stuff. It's got to be so and so. Or this way, or that." Rose began to cry.

Tressie rushed to her and put her arms around the heaving shoulders. "Whatever is wrong, Rose? Is it that Jarrad Lincolnshire? What's he done this time?"

"He's going back to England. Leaves next week." Between sobs Rose told Tressie about the mine owner's plans to set up his family in Virginia City. "And I'm afraid if she won't come back with him, I'll never see him again," she finished with a wail.

"Well, I wouldn't want to share a man with his wife, that's for darn sure," Tressie said. "But I guess you know what you want just like I do. I wish you'd think more of yourself than to let him ruin your life."

"I'd take what I can get and be grateful for it, from Jarrad Lincolnshire. I wish I didn't love him so." Rose sobbed, wiping at her eyes. She had never meant to let her feelings show so plainly. There were plenty of other men, and she could have any of them she wanted. How foolish to mourn the loss of one out of so many.

"Oh, Rose," Tressie said softly, "forget about Jarrad Lincolnshire. He has a wife and children that he loves. He uses you for his own pleasure, and when it comes right down to it, he'll choose them over you." She wondered that she could see so well what her friend should do, but her own decisions came with so much difficulty. All she knew was what she had to do, not what she ought to do.

But though she begged and pleaded, all Rose Langue knew for sure was that she was losing the man she loved because he didn't return that love. She simply couldn't admit that he had been using her for his own pleasure.

As Tressie started to take her leave, Rose remembered the blue dress and pulled it from the closet.

"Oh, Rose, would you keep it for me? When this is all over, I'll come back and get it."

Rose silently rehung the dress, then embraced and kissed her friend.

"I'm going to miss you something awful," Tressie whispered.

"Me, too, but you take care of that big man. He'll need plenty of tender loving care. He has a grieving heart, so you be good to him, you hear? And if he ain't good to you, you let me know and I'll see he pays."

Tressie nodded, but could say no more, for her throat was clogged, her heart overflowing with emotions she could hardly bear.

Fear remained beneath the anticipation and excitement, and then there was, of course, the love she felt for Reed. At the same time, leaving Caleb behind caused a new burden of grief to add to that she carried for Mama and her young'un buried on the plains. So many memories trailed behind her. All at once she wanted to be gone, even though it meant saying good-bye to Rose, the only true friend she had ever made in her adult life. It would be almost as bad as when she left her childhood home.

Would she ever see Rose again? She didn't know, but as she walked beside Rose down the long staircase, she sensed that a whole new adventure was beginning to unfold for her.

Picking her way across the muddy street, she saw Reed waiting outside the mercantile. He hurried to meet her, lifted her out of the mud, and deposited her with a laugh on the boardwalk. "Careful, girl. That quick mire will suck you right under."

He had a sparkle to his eyes, a need-to-be-gone look that brightened his sculptured features.

The feeling was contagious and she laughed back at him.

Inside, they picked out some britches and shirts from the boys' clothing in stock.

He plucked a hat from the top of a stack. "Try this. See if you can stuff those locks up under it. I hate like hell to have to cut them. Maybe we can poke 'em up, like this," he said merrily, trying to get the unruly ringlets to stay put.

She shook her head. "It's no use. If I just put my hair up, suppose my hat comes off. Everyone would see immediately. Even if I braided it. No, we have to cut it. That's the only way it'll be—" She broke off and tilted her head at the mirror. "Besides, it won't be so bad. It was short when you came to the farm. I must not have looked too awful."

"Awful? Why do you think I took off like a scalded dog the first chance I got?" he teased.

"Well, mister smarty, it wasn't because of my hair, I'd wager. Was it?" She gouged at his ribs, making him holler. "Was it?"

"Must've been your winning ways, then," he allowed in all seriousness.

"Add some shears to our supplies, if you didn't already. You can have the privilege of chopping it all off, soon as we make camp. Meanwhile, I'll just twist it up, like this."

Both were so absorbed in their plans that neither saw Dr. Gideon until he stood at the counter near where they talked. "Mrs. Majors, what a pleasure to see you," the big man boomed.

Reed, who had been looking at Tressie, whirled.

Gideon took a few steps toward them. "And your friend here. I don't believe we've met. I'm Abel Gideon. You must be the little one's daddy. He had your eyes, I believe."

Gideon glared at Reed so intently that it made him squirm. What was going on here? He'd be damned if he'd correct this man's assumptions. It was none of his business anyway.

"Reed Bannon," Reed growled, and stuck out a hand.

Gideon's nostrils flared and he ignored the hand, saying, "Sorry about your boy."

"Thank you. Are you ready to go, Tressie?"

She nodded wordlessly and followed Reed up front, where they paid for their purchases, adding a pair of scissors to the stack of clothing.

"What was that all about?" Reed said.

"I don't like him a bit. I don't think he's a very good doctor, and I wish I'd have gotten someone else for Caleb. Gideon makes me all crawly inside. He looks at me like he knows something about me he shouldn't."

"I get that same feeling. Ah, hell, I think we're just looking for troubles where there aren't any." He shrugged, and grabbed her hand. "Come on, I want to show you something you're going to love."

At the livery stable was a tiny gray donkey who stared at them with soft brown eyes, long ears swinging forward in greeting. She rubbed the soft but prickly nose. "Oh, is he ours?"

"Yep. Every stubborn foot of him. This time we go in style, darlin'. He's going to carry everything. And that's not all." He led her to a stall in which stood two horses. "This time we ride. And I bought lots of socks, too," he finished as he went to the far wall where he'd piled all their belongings.

She eyed the smaller of the two roans. "Ride? Well, I'm not very good at that. I guess you'll have to teach me." Then, unable to contain her excitement any longer, she danced into his arms. "Are we leaving soon?"

He smiled down into her ecstatic features and nodded.

The adventure was about to begin, and despite the purpose of their trip, she could hardly wait.

Six

Tressie and Reed headed west out of Virginia City, following the Ruby River. Nearby was the famed Alder Gulch strike. As far as they could see in any direction, men panned for gold.

Gaunt-framed, hung with faded flannel shirts and patched trousers, hands puffy from constant dipping in the cold streams, the gold seekers scarcely resembled men who might have in their pokes thousands of dollars worth of gold. Greasy slouch hats shaded them from the sun, but nothing would ward off extreme bouts of homesickness, dysentery, or scurvy. How could they believe it was worth it?

Fascinated, Tressie slowed her mount to study three or four men manning a cradle, rocking the wooden contraption while pouring water over gravel dumped in the hopper. Suppose one of them came up with more than a little dust settling around the riffles in the foot. What would he do if the washing uncovered a $5,000 nugget? It had been known to happen.

Yet she'd heard miners talk enough to know that many rarely did better than break even. Some not even that. Those were the ones who had given up and gone to work at mines like Lincolnshire's.

Soon Tressie and Reed entered Nevada City, a place not very different from Virginia City. Both had come to life as gold camps with the Alder Gulch strike. Slowly the pair made their way among the dirty-haired, foul-bodied men who all looked much the same. Had Papa become one of them? Would she even know him if she saw him?

For the most part, Reed asked the questions. In bars and other business establishments, she would wait outside while he inquired of the owners and customers. Had they ever run up against Evan Majors? Did he trade there, or had he ever passed through headed for somewhere else?

To every question the answer was a disinterested shrug or shake of the head.

On the trail she did the looking, giving everyone they spotted a quick once-over. And on they rode. No place could be home until they ran down Evan Majors. Until Tressie made her peace.

Near Adobe they set up their first camp. When he finally reined in his horse, she slipped from the saddle with a soft moan. The ground appeared to buckle under her and she swayed on spraddled legs. The gentle mare swung her head around as if to say, *I'm the one who does all the work, and you complain.*

She patted the sweet little animal on the rump and chuckled.

"Sore?" he asked with a crooked grin. He felt great after a day in the saddle. "Just think, at least it's not your feet that hurt."

"Oh, yes, you can laugh." She rubbed at her bottom. "I suppose you're just perfectly okay."

He threw a leg across the saddle horn and slid to the ground. "I'll have you know, ma'am, I was born in the saddle, and damn glad to get back in one, too."

"Show-off," she lifted the stirrup to unbuckle the cinch.

"I'll do that," he said. "But just this one time, and that because I feel sorry for you." With competent fingers he loosened the girth and dragged off the saddle.

She punched him lightly with a doubled-up fist. "I'll teach you to laugh at me, you lunkhead."

"Oh, yeah? When's my first lesson?"

She half turned, but the laugh that bubbled up from her throat was choked off. For a split second she caught sight of a fleeting shadow moving through the edge of the trees. On closer inspection, she could see no one was there. A finger of fear walked up her backbone as she peered into the gloom of the woods.

"What? What is it, honey?"

"I don't know. I thought... I guess it was just my imagination. Never mind, I'm just being silly. I'll be okay if you give me something to do. Shall I unpack Millie?"

She'd named the dove-gray little animal Millie despite his protest that the donkey was a jack, not a jenny. Her reply had been that she would not call such a lovable little animal Jack.

He suggested Billie, she came back with Tillie and they compromised.

All the while she laid out supplies, she continued to experience a creepy feeling that they were being watched. But as dusk turned to night and no campfire glowed nearby, she told herself her nervousness was only because she feared someone might find out she was a woman.

When Reed approached in his light-footed way, she yowled in surprise. "Don't come up on me like that. Whistle or get a bell or something."

"You mean like this?" he asked, and let out a shrill whistle that set the horses whinnying.

Before she could object, he raced to her side and grabbed her up in a bear hug. "God, it's good to be able to hold you. Doesn't it feel good?"

He was impossible, and she was soon playing light right back at him. While they were both in that mood, he cut off her curls, and it wasn't so bad. It was only a condition for keeping her safe, after all, and they were able to laugh at her shorn appearance... at least a little.

When she fetched the frying pan, he took it from her.

"Tonight you rest, I cook. After all, you are a poor pilgrim, and you need to get used to this hard life." A grin danced his features into life, but he sobered quickly. "I warn you, though, girl...." He paused, tousled her short hair. "Uh, I mean lad, you'll carry your weight after today. I'll not have any shirkers in this outfit. Besides, men don't lay around and let other men do all the work, like some women."

She launched herself at him, knocking the frying pan aside. They ended up rolling around in the dirt, tickling and shouting, finally coming to rest wrapped in each other's arms.

"What would people say about this?" she teased, kissing him lightly.

"Who cares?" He returned the kiss but much more soundly.

"They'd say," she managed when she came up for air, "that either I'm not a boy, or there's something bad wrong with you, that's what they'd say. Now let me up and let's us get respectable, at least till the fire's out."

Later that night, as they lay together wrapped in blankets to keep out the cold night air, she cried. She didn't know it was going to happen, had absolutely no warning. The hot tears just began to flow, silent as the fall of snowflakes. Worse, she couldn't tell him why. It was all wound up in Mama and Papa, the babies, the loneliness of the past few months, and the joy of being with him.

And so he held her close until she slept, wondering with dread if he was going to be able to make her happy. She had suffered so much for one so young, and he didn't know what else he could do that he hadn't already done.

She awoke before dawn and turned to snuggle against him, but the pile of blankets and the saddle where he had lain his head were empty. She sat up and rubbed at her eyes. In the wind came the smell of salt pork frying and the heavy smoke of fires. Men swarmed from one gold camp to another and camped everywhere in search of the sun-bright ore. How would she ever determine Papa's whereabouts? It would have been easier to find him in a city like St. Louis, where folks pretty much stayed put. This immense country was fairly crawling with prospectors who moved on at the least whim.

Before day broke she struggled into her boots and hightailed it for the woods. Maintaining the facade of being male was harder than she'd thought it would be, for eyes could be anywhere and boys did their private business in a much different way than girls.

Squatted in the bushes, britches down around her ankles, she couldn't suppress a giggle. She guessed men did have to do it this way at least once in a while, but how easy it was for them the rest of the time. Just unzip and let 'er fly.

She arrived back at camp about the same time as he did, and together they built up the fire and cooked breakfast.

Sopping up the last of her mush with a sourdough biscuit, Tressie said, "There's a lot more prospectors than I expected. Do you think we'll ever find him?"

He shrugged. "Well, we can sure say we gave it our best. If he's here to find, we'll find him. If not, well then, we'll just… just get on with it, I reckon."

"With what?" she asked, giving him a squared-on look.

"Why, our lives, of course." He paused in his chewing and eyed her steadily. What did she mean by that? Had she changed her mind?

"I don't mean that. I mean, what are we going to do? Homestead some land, get jobs in town, prospect? We don't either one exactly have a calling."

The insistent question brought him a feeling of relief, and he let out a sigh. "Well, I know how to ride; I've worked for a freighting company. With this country growing like it is, there'll be a great need for moving things from one place to the other. I'm afraid I wouldn't make much of a farmer, though."

She set her tin plate down and picked up a cup of steaming, black-as-mud coffee. "Then you'd like to stay here, in the mountains?"

"I expect." He looked up. "Unless you'd like to go elsewhere. With the war over, these boomtowns will likely become permanent settlements. There'll be churches and schools as well as businesses of every description. Hell, look at Virginia City already. The world is marching West, Tressie, and we're already here."

She nodded, his excitement catching hold of her. The only other place she would want to live would be in the Missouri Ozarks, but what with all her people gone on, these mountains would suit her just as well.

"Maybe we'll strike gold," she said with an impish grin. "And then we'll be rich and we can go anywhere we want and live anywhere we want."

"That's a fair dream," He rose. "Time we broke camp. Oh, I made an early morning round asking questions. A feller camped yonder"—he pointed toward a draw—"he said he run up against a man name of Majors a few months back. Panning down near the Bitterroots. I thought we might head that way."

"Oh, why didn't you tell me earlier? Did he say it was Papa? Did he talk to him? Was he…was he okay?"

Not wanting to turn around and see her face, he stopped and hung his head for a moment. Hate and love all tangled up with vengeance could do a lot of damage to all involved. His own pa's actions had come near ruining Reed's life, had chased him from one place to another like a pursuing demon. But she didn't see that yet.

He drew in a deep breath, said softly, "Now, Tressie, don't go getting your hopes up. He couldn't remember if that was his first name or last, nor much about him, except that he thought he hailed from the high plains. That's the onliest reason I'd say we even try to find him. It could be a wild goose chase, and I think we should keep checking out every man we meet, not just rush off after this one."

This was true, but still she couldn't help being anxious to learn more. "Where is this Bitterroot? And how would we go about finding his claim after we got there?"

"Bitterroot Mountains. Assayer's or claims office in the nearest town, I would reckon," he muttered. The tone of her questions just plain scared him. His sweet little gal turning all mean and single-purposed lent a dread to his own soul. He had no solutions, though. In his experience, folks had to do what they had to do.

"Well, then, let's get moving," she said, and started cleaning up their breakfast things while he packed and saddled their mounts.

At Twin Bridges she took the time to write to Rose Langue, explaining what they had learned and where they were headed. She left it for the eastbound stage.

They spent the night outside of town and the next morning headed south for Dillon, the next settlement of any size. Reed had grown just plain grumpy as the days wore on. He even took to sleeping across the fire from her. Or if she complained of the cold and moved to his side, he would turn his back, presenting his stiff haunches for her to warm up on. Having come up with no cure for her problems, Reed felt helpless and that made him angry. Why was he so danged scared to assert himself? Be a man? He feared he knew the answer to that.

She resented being at the mercy of this man's changing moods, and she'd be darned if she'd beg him to talk to or put his arms around her. If he had a mad on, then let him keep it.

Besides, they were hot on Papa's trail, and she had other things to occupy her thoughts—like what would she do if she walked up on him face-to-face? She'd supposed a confrontation would mean she could vent all her hate. Watch his face crumple in shame when he learned what his leaving had caused. Now she wasn't so sure.

The trail wound deeper into the mountains and grew more steep and difficult. On the third night out after learning Papa might be in the Bitterroot Mountains south of Dillon, Reed had had enough talk about what she would say and do to the man. He decided to tell her so and to hell with the consequences.

After supper that evening he brought up the subject. Then he like to not got started, his tongue was so tied up. He picked at his teeth, shifted from sitting cross-legged to leaning back with his head on his saddle, then back to a sit.

"Something bothering you?" she asked. "You're acting like you've sat on an anthill or something."

"I was just thinking about—"

"You seem to be doing a lot of that lately, and little else," she snapped.

"I expect I have. Girl, have you changed your mind?"

"Changed my mind about what?" Tressie drew lines in the dirt, then gazed at the fire. She could feel him looking at her, his gaze boring icy holes in her flesh.

"About us." A short, barked retort that was the closest he ever came to raising his voice in anger.

"Well, I have to admit, thinking about being around someone who can go for a week without so much as a *good morning, dear*, does give me pause."

He snorted. "That isn't what I meant, and you know it. Do you wish you could take back your promises to me so you could concentrate on paying back your pa, if and when we find him?"

She swirled the stick and flipped a cloud of dust into the fire. Torn between love and hate, she was utterly miserable. She wanted to trust this man, yet all she could think about when she looked at him was Papa's betrayal. Creeping ever into her thoughts was the question, would he desert her, too? If she trusted him too much, left herself at his mercy, would she one day wake up to find him gone? Such doubts put their love in peril and caused her to question many of her own motives.

"It just isn't fair," she wailed at last. "I love you, Reed. With all my heart. But when I… when you said… oh, darn it, help me."

He stared into the fire, his somber eyes darker than the night and glinting with moisture. "I can't help you on this one, Tressie, girl. This is exactly why I wouldn't just grab you up and run away with you, though Lord knows I've wanted to enough times. And then I think of all the times I've run away when the going got tough. I think of seeing that faraway glint come into your eye when you think of your pa, and I get scared. Scared of what you'll do, scared of what I'll do."

She had begun to cry softly. "You won't just leave me out here all alone, will you?"

The poor little thing. He cleared his burning throat, wanted to take her in his arms, do his best to convince her that their love was stronger than his cowardice or her need for revenge.

All he could do was say brokenly, "I swear I'll stick by you, Tressie. I'm so tired of running. But I understand how you feel, I truly do. I just wish…well, hell, I wish we could."

"Then quit acting like you're mad at me all the time. It's awful lonely riding all day every day without a word out of you."

"I'm not mad at you. I just can't take… touching you, being around and knowing that we can't… I love you, Tressie, and I don't want to hurt you. I promised I'd help you find your pa, and I will. But dang it, girl, you're gonna have to quit snuggling up to me. Till this is over and we get married, things between us will have to be strictly business. Or we can forget all this and make us a life."

She gazed longingly into his moist dark eyes, saw the love and goodness there, and almost gave in. But she couldn't. She kept remembering her mama crying night after night, remembered her own pain at being abandoned, and then the worst thing of all when Mama lay in labor screaming out Papa's name over and over, and him not there. No. She would not give up. She shook her head slowly.

"I can't have a life till I find Papa. Till I can see his face when I tell him what he did. How much he hurt Mama and me. No matter what we did or where we went, I'd always think about it. And you're right. It'll eat me alive, and so I have to find him. Get rid of the pain and the hate. I loved him so much. I love you so much. Can't you understand what I'm saying? Please be patient. Please."

In a strange sort of way he sympathized with her, even though he didn't understand her decision. It cut deeply into his heart until he wanted to throw something, or ball his fists and scream his disappointment to the heavens. Instead, he said in a flat voice:

"Well, if you can't give up this crazy idea of yours that you have to pay back your pa for what he did, then you're not ready for a life of your own. Hell, maybe I'm not, either, now that I think on it.

"One thing's for sure, we can't keep rolling around in bed together. It ain't right, and besides, ain't no telling what could happen; then what would we do?"

She stared at the ground .He was right. A lump swelled in her throat that she couldn't swallow past. If she gave up looking for Papa and married him, they could have a life out here in the mountains, or go farther west. It was a wonderful fantasy.

She grinned a sad little grin. "Okay, but when it's cold can I sleep with you?"

"Dammit, girl, that's asking too much. Just get closer to the blamed fire if you're cold." It was the harshest tone he'd ever used with her, and he felt terrible when the words tumbled past his tongue. But a man could only be tempted so far.

As summer wore on and they rode in and out of gatherings

of prospectors who all had the same answers to their questions about Evan Majors, Reed and Tressie developed a camaraderie that extended beyond their sexual and emotional feelings for each other. Reed had kept his promise to talk to Tressie, and she was like a child who went to bed on an argument and upon wakening forgot all about it. They were friends, at ease with each other, and it felt good.

Occasionally she would ask, "How much farther to Dillon?"

And he would reply patiently, almost always the same answer, "We'll just have to ride till we get there. I haven't been over this way in years. Besides, these gold strike towns have sprung up where once there was nothing."

Another time she asked, "Where did you live when you were a little boy?"

That set him off on another tale. "Oh, we were plains Sioux. These mountains were too tough for wintering. This is where the gods live."

Tressie looked out across the panorama of rugged peaks, deep valleys, and gigantic pine reaching for the sky. "I'm not surprised. The gods sure did know what they were doing, saving this for themselves."

They had been following a downward trail all day, and she soon grew weary of such a challenge to her meager riding skills. It was hard not to hang on to the horn, a thing he had cautioned her more than once not to do.

"It makes the animal's shoulders sore after a while," he told her every time he noticed her hands bunched over the horn during a particularly sheer descent. "Use the stirrups to hold yourself. Sit back easy and balance on the balls of your feet. Your mount knows what she's doing."

"It wouldn't be so hard if I couldn't see where we'll fall if she stumbles." Climbing had been a lot easier.

"We could tie your bandanna around your eyes." He couldn't help laughing.

After a while, she responded, "No, I guess I wouldn't like that, either."

Once they took a cold noonday meal sitting on a huge boulder on an overhang that gave them a bird's-eye view of a distant river valley. Virgin long-needled pine clung to the steep and rocky incline. Just below the swaying tops were clusters of brown cones.

"This must be what a bird feels like," Tressie said. "I could almost reach down and pluck one out of the tree-top.

"Better not. You'd roll for a hundred miles if you lost your balance." She breathed deeply of the sweet air. "Isn't it lovely?"

Wildflowers of every color and description sprouted from seams in the hard rock. Overhead their blossoms swayed in the gentle breeze, hanging upside down as if it were a quite natural condition. Reds and purples, whites and yellows, the blooms exuded a luscious fragrance that sweetened the mountain air.

Suddenly she heard something—a branch cracking, rocks scattering—and she stiffened. "Reed."

He held up a hand. "I heard. Be still."

The mare danced and rattled gravel underfoot; Millie curled her lip to reveal long teeth and emit what could only be called a laugh. His large roan gelding called out shrilly. There was an answering whinny.

"Someone coming up the trail," he said. "What will we do?"

He glanced at her and saw that she was afraid. "Do? Why, nothing. We're out here. It stands to reason others are, too, and with no more underhanded motives than we have. We'll stay to the side until they pass; the trail is narrow."

"Are we meeting them or are they coming up on us?"

He cocked his head. "In this country, it's hard to tell, but I think it came from down yonder behind us."

She shuddered. Something about another rider on their back trail bothered her, as if someone were spying on them.

That, of course, was silly. But she had never shaken the earlier feeling that they were being watched. It came and went with regularity, though she'd actually never seen anyone.

Both listened intently for quite a while, but nothing more was heard. No rider or his animal. Finally Reed shrugged and slid off the boulder. "That's funny. I didn't notice a way off this goat trail the way we came. Ah, well. Sound travels strange up here in this thin air. Could have been down below on another trail, I suppose."

He sounded puzzled, and that bothered her. He made few mistakes on the trail. If he said someone was riding up on them, then it was probably true. So why hadn't that person come on? There was only one reason that she could think of, and that was that the person on their trail was staying behind them deliberately. Following. Spying.

It was nearly dark before they found a place to camp for the night, and both were kept busy until after they settled down to eat their meal. He had chosen a stand of pine nested up against a steep outcropping of sienna-colored rocks the size of ships. Back off the main trail a ways, the needle-covered ground offered a soft bed, the heavy branches overhead a shelter from the chilling dew that fell nightly. They carried plenty of water, but a plus for this campsite was the small spring bubbling from a crevice in the rocks to run merrily over moss-covered gravel and spill noisily down the side of the mountain.

They ate hungrily and in silence until Reed opened a can of fruit with his knife. Spooning up a golden peach, he sucked at the sugary syrup. "Couldn't resist buying these. Nothing better than peaches from a can. Too bad we couldn't bring more."

"It's time we had a treat. Back home we grew these on trees." She tasted her own, licked her lips. "Good, all right, but if you think these are good, you ought to have tasted ours. I still miss home." She decided she didn't want to talk about that anymore and said, "If we'd stay in one place long enough, I'd cook up some of those dry beans."

"There'll be time for that later," he said.

"When we get where we're going," she said like an echo. "I wish——" "No more than I do, sweetheart. No more than I do."

"Yes. Well, if you don't mind, that water is mighty tempting. I think I'll take a bath."

He slurped up the rest of the thick juice and put his plate down. "And I think I'll just take a look around. Check things out a bit. You need me, just give a holler."

He had no intention of sticking around to watch her bathe, not with things the way they were. Besides, he wanted to check out their back trail. Ever since hearing that horse whinny earlier in the day, he'd expected someone to ride up on them. Or at least to hear other signs of a traveler. But there'd been nothing, and that was plumb strange.

For the first time since setting out from Virginia City, he pulled his rifle from the scabbard. She noticed him going armed to scout the area. So he was taking their earlier mysterious visitor seriously.

In the gathering darkness she fetched a bar of soap and went to the spring. There she sat to remove her boots, then slipped out of her men's britches and flannel shirt. Both smelled of sweat and the trail. She would wash them after she bathed. Standing, she unwrapped the tight binding from around her chest. She stretched, pale skin glowing in the half-light. For a moment she rubbed her hands over the itchy flesh of her breasts and squirmed when the nipples puckered.

She wanted to make love to him, and the thought caused all kinds of problems with her young body. Ignoring the pain/pleasure urges, she bent to wet the bar of soap and began to lather it over one ankle and calf.

In the utter stillness someone giggled. She heard it distinctly and whirled, soap cupped in both hands between her breasts. Reed couldn't giggle like that if he had to. A stranger was watching her.

She shouted Reed's name as loud as she could, at the same time charging for the camp and something to cover herself with. She had almost reached the pile of blankets when the shadowy figures stepped from behind the trees like ghosts magically becoming visible. There were seven of them, and they looked to be no more than fifteen or so. Indian boys wearing very little clothing. The light from the campfire set their naked bodies to gleaming as if they were coated in grease. Perhaps they were.

She stopped in midstride. Unable to get to the blankets, she turned to go the other way where she could hide. One of the boys yipped and leaped quickly into her path. She screeched again, and the soap went flying from her hands. The boys really thought that was funny. They kept shouting curt words to each other, nodding and laughing. One cupped his hands over his crotch in a crude gesture. That they found even funnier.

The boy nearest her moved quickly and grabbed her by the arm. She jerked away, shouted, "No!"

He smacked her with the flat of his palm between her breasts and repeated the word "No!" sharp as a rifle's fire. The blow jarred her teeth and she staggered backward.

Eyes flitting from one looming shadow to another, she screamed Reed's name once again.

Where was he? Was he going to let these savages have their way with her? They were only boys, but their intention was obvious. They wanted to do more than just play games.

The boy who had smacked her reached for her hair. She dodged and he raised the other hand as if to hit her, so she stood still. He filled his fist with her short locks and shook until her teeth rattled. Immediately he gestured toward her breasts. The question became evident.

"I cut it," she whimpered. With two fingers she made a

sign for scissors and held it to her head. "Now let me go, you indecent little savage, before I give you a lesson in manners." She couldn't have explained why she said that. They didn't understand her, that was evident, but it felt good to stand up to them nevertheless.

From out of the darkness came a low, steady voice. "No, let me." The demand was followed by a sharp retort from the rifle. The bullet chipped at the trunk of a pine inches from her tormentor's head.

Reed tried out his Sioux on the boys, ordering them to leave his woman be, followed by a vivid description of what he would do to their private parts if they didn't. Later he wasn't sure if it was the gun or his words that sent the young braves on their way. They'd evidently hidden their horses up the trail, for soon after they lit out, the pounding of hooves signaled their departure.

She stood there a moment, rubbing at her aching head and trying to catch her breath. When she did, it was to turn on Reed. "Where were you? What took you so long? Those nasty little savages could have killed me."

It was so dark under the pines that only the firelight revealed her naked body. And he was halfway through answering her accusation when he pivoted from watching the boys leave.

"At least we know who we heard earlier—" Catching sight of her drove the rest of his reply from his mouth. Taking one giant stride, he folded her up in his arms, kissed her long and hard, then pushed her away.

She scarcely responded to the kiss before it was over. She held the back of her hand to her mouth, tears glistening in her green eyes, and struggled against the swell of passion in her loins. "Reed, I—"

"Put some clothes on now, before someone sees you," he said.

It took all the willpower he had to walk away from her, standing there with her arms stiffly at her sides, the glory of her exquisite body open to the shadow and light thrown by the flickering fire. He wanted her as badly as he ever had wanted anyone or anything in his entire life. There were times when he thought he could make her choose between him and her need for vengeance, but he couldn't bring himself to do it. So he would just walk away, like always.

Seven

That summer of 1865, Rose Langue wasn't sure whose leaving devastated her more, Jarrad's or Tressie's. Her life had been forever changed by both. Jarrad she cursed for making her fall in love with him then totally disregarding her feelings; Tressie she blessed for showing her that youth and courage and beauty of soul still counted for something in this jaded old world.

Once Jarrad Lincolnshire took the stagecoach east where he would board a ship for England, Rose found other men boring, infantile, and most of all dreadfully depressing. She finally quit dealing with them altogether, letting the hurdy-gurdy house and girls like Maggie earn money for her. There was no place where Rose felt entirely comfortable anymore. On Jarrad Lincolnshire's arm, her presence had been accepted in places like the theater and the posh eating establishments in town.

Virginia City continued to grow, becoming more and more sophisticated. Families moved in, which meant the influx of women and children other than the wives of rich merchants and miners. A middle class had developed, and for that schools and churches were needed.

Rose would have liked to attend church services and mingle with these wives and mothers, but of course she couldn't. So she had herself a small house built on the outskirts of town somewhat removed from the Golden Sun. Out back she began a flower garden and hired the son of the Chinese launderer to help out. He would carry bucket after bucket of water to her tender new roses, plants that had been shipped on the stage all the way from St. Louis. The day the first delicate pale pink petals of the pampered Radiance rose unfolded, she buried her nose in the fragrant flower and cried. How rare to have had a hand in bringing such beauty to this raw and ugly town.

Soon she had not only roses, but a variety of blooming shrubs, including the gracious mountain laurel. By the following spring she hoped to see lilies, jonquils and tulips, bulbs she had already ordered from Pennsylvania.

One day in early August she left her little garden and went in the house by the back entrance just as someone tapped on the front door. She had grown accustomed to an occasional visit from one of the girls at the Golden Sun, who on their time off liked to visit her rose garden and take a glass of lemonade with their friend and employer. She encouraged such visits, for they filled a corner of her lonely life.

Wiping perspiration from her face and pulling off her work gloves, she opened the door. To her surprise a young man stood there, rumpled black hat in hand, a nervous smile playing around his finely drawn lips. He tipped his head forward slightly in a nod, loosening golden hair that fell over his ears. "Ma'am? I'm sorry to bother you, but I was told to bring this to you."

"What?" she asked, seeing nothing but the hat held in both hands across his belt.

Obviously flustered, he met her gaze squarely while flashing snowy white teeth and digging around in his pockets. "It's here, somewhere."

Rose couldn't help but return his smile. For some reason she had always had this effect on men, and she had grown to accept it and take advantage of it. Lately such thoughts had not entered her mind. She grieved for Jarrad as if he had died, and a widow in mourning did not raise her eyes to those of other gentlemen. But this one…well, he was a most impressive young man. Noteworthy.

He continued to finger through the pockets of his black pants until he finally came up with a flat package wrapped carefully in brown paper. He held it out to her, blushing furiously when her fingers brushed his in passing.

"What is this?"

"A tintype, ma'am."

She picked at the string with long fingernails. "I'm afraid I can't untie this knot. Won't you come in?" She stepped back out of the doorway, still studying the parcel. "Would you like some lemonade? And I'll let you unfasten this while I fetch it."

The young man glanced around at the charming room with pink and white chintz curtains that matched throw covers on the delicate furniture, at the exquisite hand-painted glass shades on the kerosene lamps, at the dainty doilies and antimacassars, and he shuffled his booted feet.

"I don't know, ma'am. I couldn't rightly set on any of this fine furniture. I might mess it up."

Rose laughed heartily. "Well, then, if you're a country boy, why don't you just come with me out to the kitchen? I think we'd both feel more at home there. And the chairs are sturdier."

Without waiting for an answer, she regally led the way through the arched doorway into a yellow and white kitchen. Sunlight splashed three windows that framed the lovely rose garden out back. The young man gasped with delight.

"You like it?" she asked, and fetched a pitcher of lemonade from the wooden box alongside the dry sink. She knelt and unwrapped a block of ice in the bottom of the box, chipping off several slivers for each of two glasses, which she then filled to the top with frosty, shimmering lemonade.

"You'd never know coming up on it from outside that it would be so…so, well…so womany," he said.

She dimpled with pleasure at the compliment and handed him his glass. "What's your name, and who sent you here with that?" She gestured at the packet now lying on the oiled tabletop.

He cleared his throat, as if only now remembering his mission. "Uh, well, I'm Ben Poole, and I—" He broke off and took a sip of the cold drink. "Ramey, over at the Busted Mule, he said you would want to see this." The boy gestured at the still-wrapped package.

"Well, then, I'd appreciate it if you would unwrap it for me," Rose said, and sat in one of the two chairs. "Sit, Ben. Sit, and show me what you've got."

It was a hot day, and perspiration ran from under Rose's heavy golden hair, piled high in enormous curls. She plucked a wisp of white linen from her bodice and blotted the moisture at her throat and across the swelling of her breasts peeking from the low-cut neckline.

Ben Poole blushed again and tried to take his eyes from her long enough to untie the knot on the small package. He was having a very hard time doing either.

She felt a certain amount of pity for the young man, who obviously hadn't been around any women save his own mother. He no doubt was the victim of rampaging desires he had no idea what to do with. He was certainly at that age, maybe sixteen or seventeen. He could very well have been her son.

"Ben, show me the picture. Then I want you to go over to the Golden Sun, tell Maggie I sent you especially to her. She'll be good for you, son. Take care of those urges you're experiencing. You don't want me, I'm old enough to be your mother. And besides, I'm retired. Maggie, she's just about right. She can show you things you've only imagined, if that. And you tell her, Ben, that she's paid. I'll take care of it."

As Rose spoke she looked straight into the boy's dark blue eyes, saw a flare of desire there, then the embarrassment quickly covered by the lowering of his long, dark lashes.

Ben went to work diligently and soon had the string off. He handed the package to Rose without unwrapping the paper or meeting her steady gaze.

"Thank you kindly, Ben. Now, finish your lemonade and you can go."

He took a long two or three gulps, then asked, "Maggie?"

"Yes, that's right. And thank you for this."

Ben took another sip, then snapped his fingers. "Oh, Ramey, he said to tell you that if you wanted to know anything about that, you should come see him. Said some fella turned up with it, tried to use it as stakes in a poker game. Ramey, he knew you would be interested, seeing as how you was friends with this girl."

Rose's heart leaped into her throat and she ripped back the paper. There, in shades of sienna and cream preserved for all time, was the likeness of Tressie Majors with an older woman. The girl's hair hung in the long curls of childhood, adding a certain innocence to the familiar features, but it was Tressie, perhaps at the age of fifteen or so, and probably her mother.

"Who had this, do you know?" Rose felt faint, the tight corset squeezing at her until she could scarcely breathe.

"Look on the back, ma'am. See, there, Ramey said it says something, I forget what."

Scrawled in black ink on the back of the tintype were the words "Beloved Almyra and Tressie."

"Oh, my goodness," Rose whispered. "Oh, my dear goodness. It must have belonged to Evan Majors."

"Majors, ma'am?"

Rose glanced up at the boy. "Oh, never mind. Ben, you run along, now. And don't forget Maggie, won't you? Run along. And thank you. Thank you so much."

Ben stood, downed the last swallows of lemonade in noisy gulps, and hurried from the room. Long after the front door banged closed Rose sat there staring unseeing out the windows into her rose garden.

"But where did he get it, Ramey?" Rose asked the owner of the Busted Mule that very same afternoon. She hadn't even waited for Ben to get out of sight on the street in front of her house before heading for the gambling saloon.

"Oh, he had a story to tell, all right, and it's a doozy. Near as I remember he found it on the dead body of a prospector down around Sugar Flats. That's near the divide."

She nodded impatiently. "I know where Sugar Flats is. The man he found it on. Was he a tall fella, brown hair?"

"Nah, he said he was an old codger, bald with lots of whiskers. Reason I remember, he was a laughing about this old prospector being so old he probably just died of old age right in the midst of what he was doing. You know, took one step, fell down the next?"

"Did he have a name?"

"Who?" Ramey asked, and poured them each a mug of dark beer. "The old prospector, who else?"

Ramey frowned. "Fella didn't say. You sure are het up over this, Rose. It's only a likeness of that gal what cooked up at the Lincolnshire Mines last winter. What ever become of her, anyways?"

"She rode out to hunt for her lost pa. Did you read the back of this?"

"Yep, I did." Ramey's close-set brown eyes sparked. "Say, you thinking that old prospector was this little gal's pa, dead and gone on?"

"Of course not. Evan was...is a younger man. But where did this old man get the tintype, Ramey? That's what I want to know. Is this fella that had it still in town?"

Ramey shrugged. "Beats me. Tossed him outta here when he

run out a money and started making such a fuss over us not using that there for ante. You might try up at the mine. He muttered something about getting himself a job to get a stake. Onliest place I know of a man dumb as a stump can earn him some wages."

She finished her beer. "Thanks, Ramey. I appreciate this. That boy, Ben Poole? Where'd he come in from, do you know?"

"Purdy good kid, ain't he? Come up from down South somewheres. Served in the last year or so of the war down there. His people was all massacred, so when the war finished up, he just got on his horse and rode. He tole me he just rode till he couldn't hang on no more, then slid off into the dirt. And that's what he looked like when he come in here, too. Flat rode to a frazzle. I needed a boy to sweep up, so I hired him."

"But he's only fifteen, maybe sixteen years old. He served in the war a year?"

"Oh, hell, yes. Along at the last they had kids no older'n twelve taking up arms. Those was desperate days for the Confederacy, I reckon." Ramey took her mug and rubbed at the bar with a rag. "Damn glad that hellish killing war come to a end. Such pure foolishness. Killed off too many of our young'uns. And fer what? I ask you that, Rose, fer what?"

"It's been my experience, Ramey, that man will always fight man, one way or another. It's just in their nature, like they were born with a killing club in their hands or something. There'll be other things to fight over, I'd wager. Well, I think I'll ride on up to the mine and see what I can learn. You be good to that Ben Poole, you hear me? I hear you're not, I'll take him away from you. I could use me a good-looking swamper. My girls'd treat him real good, too."

Ramey chuckled. "Hell, Rose, they'll treat him real good anyways. Good luck to you."

She thanked Ramey and stepped from the darkness of the saloon out into the blazing afternoon heat.

Her next stop was the livery stable, and she waited impatiently while Grainger harnessed her black mare to the small buggy. Then she thanked him, let him help her up into the seat, and headed for the Lincolnshire Mines.

This part was not going to be easy. She hadn't gone near the place since Jarrad had left back in late April, and doing so now, she feared, would bring back many painful memories. But she'd set herself a task and she had no intention of backing out. If Evan Majors was dead, Tressie needed to know it, but she certainly didn't need rumors of his death to add to her troubles.

The last she had heard from her friend was a letter that said she and Reed were headed south to Dillon and on to Lima in the Bitterroot Mountains. Rose intended to run down the man who showed up in Virginia City carrying a tintype of Tressie and her ma. Maybe she could bring an end to this fruitless search of Tressie's. At least that sweet girl could find happiness, even if it wasn't in the cards for Rose.

Hauling at the reins, she stopped the horse outside the office of the Lincolnshire Mines. She could almost imagine the gangly Englishman bursting through the door, holding out his arms to her, lifting her down and embracing her.

Tears pooled in her eyes and overflowed the corners. She wiped at them angrily. It was time she got over the hurt of losing Jarrad to that upper-class snob of a wife who considered herself too good for this country.

Jarrad's bookkeeper looked up from his desk when Rose walked in. He was a little bit of a man with a bald head and prissy mannerisms. His mouth was forever pursed as if he'd tasted something bitter.

"Well, Miss Rose, we haven't seen you in a while," he said in a high voice. He must wear his pants too tight.

"Hello, James."

The man stared up at her as if wishing she weren't there,

but too wary of his station to say so. "Could I perhaps help you with something?"

"Yes, I hope so. Did you hire a man this morning? A little the worse for wear and desperate for a job."

James raised his pen from the open ledger. "They're all that way, ma'am. What was his name?"

"I don't know. You can't have hired a dozen, so it couldn't be too hard for you simply to answer my question," she said sharply. She resented the condescending manner in which this little man had always treated her.

He blinked like an owl, but answered her question. "We hired two today, I believe." "And where might I find them?"

He smiled. "Up on the side of the mountain, working. Otherwise, they'll be fired come suppertime."

Rose sighed. Dealing with this man was frustrating and she resisted an urge to shake his misshapen teeth from his parsimonious little mouth. "Do you know their names?"

"Of course," he said, and stared at her.

"Have you heard from Jarrad?" Rose asked sweetly, taking another step into the room.

The man had no way of knowing the status of that relationship, despite Jarrad's having made no secret of the reason for his trip abroad. For all James knew, Jarrad and Rose would take right up where they left off when he returned, with or without his wife. So he probably better watch his step with this trollop.

"I believe he's returning within the month," James said. He took a deep breath. "One's named Phonse Cray, the other is Will O'Shaunessy. I believe the one you want is Mr. Cray. Will worked for us up until last month and just returned, so you would know him, probably. Cray is a stranger in these parts. He rode up from Sugar Flats, I believe."

"He's the one," she said, catching her breath.

"Well, I'm afraid you'll have to wait until the whistle blows. That'll be eight o'clock. Perhaps I could tell him you wish to see him."

Rose glanced around, sensing the presence of Jarrad Lincolnshire in every piece of burnished furniture in the room, in the paintings on the wall and the tidy placement of things on his desk. "Did he say if he was bringing Victoria and the girls with him?" Rose asked softly.

"I'm afraid he did," James said with a sniff. "'I'm surprised he didn't let you know. Mr. Lincolnshire is bringing the missus and the youngest daughter. The eldest married a while back. He only wired to say when they would arrive and ask that we obtain a place for them in Widow Mooney's rooming house until he can make other arrangements."

James watched her closely and she held her chin high, determined he wouldn't know that her heart had just broken into a million pieces. She hadn't known until that very moment how much hope still dwelled within her. It was one thing to carry on an affair with a married man whose wife was conspicuously absent, quite another when she lived near at hand.

"Will that be all?" James asked when she continued to stare at him.

"What? Oh, yes, James. That will be quite all. Cray, you said? I'd appreciate it if you would ask him to call on me tonight. It's most important."

"I can do that." The little ferret smirked.

She slammed from the office. She'd like to shake the hateful little sneak till his teeth rattled.

Anger drove her. So Jarrad was returning with Victoria on his arm. How long, she wondered, would that arrangement last? Well, it was definitely over. She'd not satisfy his lustful appetite while he kept that woman in a style she would demand while offering nothing in return. At least a prostitute was honest. She gave for what she got, up front. Wives, on the other hand, held out for what they wanted, giving grudgingly and making sure their husbands knew how it pained them.

She lashed at the mare with her whip, hanging on when the buggy jerked into motion.

Cray arrived at close to nine o'clock, when remnants of the summer sun touched fingers of purple clouds with brilliant orange fire. A fire in the sky that faded into darkness as Rose and he spoke, sitting at the kitchen table where earlier she had entertained young Ben Poole.

The man Cray, who said his first name was Phonse, was a soft-spoken man whose life's work would be to fail at everything he tried. That was so evident in his manner that she felt immediately sorry for him. The tale he told excited her enormously, though.

He spoke like a storyteller, as so many of his ilk, and she listened closely to what he said: "It was along about dusk when I rides up on this poor old fellow. Lying like he was sleeping beside a fire he hadn't yet built. I'd been doing some prospecting myself, see, over Dutch Oven way. So I welcomed a friendly face, maybe share some grub. When I turned him over, I saw he was dead, his eyes all bulging near out of his head, his tongue hanging out his mouth. There weren't no one around. If he had a mule it had wandered off with some of his stuff. I found that "—he gestured at the tintype that Rose had placed between them on the table— "and some other stuff. But nothing worth much, you understand."

She felt disappointment. "Is that all?"

"I didn't take nothin' valuable, I said."

"I'm not saying you did. I'm looking for the man this belonged to. I don't care what you did or didn't take. Evan Majors is his name, and I need desperately to know how to find him. He would have been carrying this picture, you see. How did this old man get it? Where had he been? If he had other things, we might be able to find out. You could help me. I'd be most grateful." She eyed him carefully.

He moistened his thick lips and leered at her.

"With money," she said quickly. "I'd pay well for the information."

"Sure," he muttered, the leer fading. "Well, I could use some gold."

"Oh, it'd be gold," Rose said quickly.

"How much?"

Rose studied him. Did he know something or was he simply trying to swindle her out of what he could?

"Depends on what you have. You show me, tell me what you know, and I'll pay you what it's worth. You can ask around; I'm an honest woman, and I wouldn't cheat you. Not someone like you."

"They ain't no law can do nothin' to me, even if you was to tell. I'd just say you was lying, you see?"

Rose clenched her fingers together in her lap and nodded somberly. "I think you can understand that I don't hold much with the law."

Cray laughed and rubbed under his nose with a grubby finger. "I reckon I know what you mean. Well, he weren't dead when I found him, you see. Truth is I met the old codger right out of Copper Springs a ways. He'd been working at one of them mines they dig right in the side of the mountain? With this feller who had that picture. Feller also had him quite a cache of gold, and he told the old man all about hisself over the time they worked together, you see. Men get like that, lonely, you see. Anyways, they got close, and traded secrets. You know how it is: If I die you get my found, if you die I get your'n? Me, I don't never tell no one nothing. I die, mine can rot right along with me, seeing as how I ain't never got nothin'.

"Anyways, this old man had got what belonged to the other

fella, and now he was a fixin' to tell me all about it so if he died I could get it. He'd buried it near his camp, you see."

Rose couldn't wait for the drawn-out tale to continue. "He got what belonged to Evan because Evan died?"

"Lady, I don't know who Evan is. This fella had this"—he pointed at Tressie's picture—"the mine caved in on him and some others. So the old man took all his belongings and lit out. He said he didn't like working in no blamed cave, anyway. Would rather set on a creek bank and pan gold as to be buried like some damned mole."

She drew in a deep breath and let it out slowly. At last. If this story was true—

She glanced at Cray. "What other belongings were there?"

"Hey, that ain't none of your business. You got what you want. I ain't giving you no more." "I ain't... I'm not asking for them. I only would want to look, make sure that this is the man I'm looking for."

"Well, you ain't gonna. I told you the truth of it. Afore he died the old man give me everthing of his and the other fellas, and I aim to keep it. You said you'd pay me, now I want my gold." Cray slammed a gnarly fist on the table, making the muted likeness of Tressie and her ma jitter.

She jumped and rose from her chair. "I'll get it for you."

She went in her bedroom, glanced at the door to make sure the man couldn't see her, and dug out her cache of gold from its hiding place in a secret drawer behind her nightstand. She removed several nuggets and replaced the heavily laden pouch with care.

Her heart battered at her rib cage so hard she could scarcely breathe. If only she could get the man to tell her a few more facts, but it would seem to be enough that Evan Majors had been the man killed in the cave-in—if this man wasn't still lying, that is.

But he probably wasn't. How could he have come up

with the name so close to Majors' if it was a lie? She chose to believe him.

She lay the nuggets near the man's hand curled on the tabletop. He stared goggle-eyed, and when he reached for them, she covered two. "Did the old man tell you anything else about this friend? Where he was from, how long he'd been out here, his name?"

Cray obviously considered his chances of taking the nuggets from her before answering. "Alls I remember is that he had a name like one of them fellas in the Army. Not colonel or captain, but something like that."

"Major, or perhaps Majors?" Rose asked.

"That were it. That right there were it. Now, can I have them?" He clutched three nuggets tightly and eyed her pale hand covering the other two. He was about to grab them.

Rose slid both across the table and stood. She could hardly wait for her visitor to leave so she could write a letter to Tressie. God, she hoped it would reach her, traveling in the wilds of the mountains. It had to, it just had to. Rose could think of nothing more important than letting Tressie know that she could end her wild vendetta, begin her life with that nice Reed Bannon.

How strange that the news of a death could carry with it so much promise. Just thinking about it gave Rose hope for her own happiness. One thing she knew for sure, she wouldn't find it with Jarrad Lincolnshire or any other man like him. She just might find it within herself.

Anyway, she felt as if she could finally seek the serenity of a fulfilling life.

Eight

Outside Dillon, at the junction of Beaverhead River and Rattlesnake Creek, Tressie and Reed discovered the sign, all but grown over in weeds and sagging badly. She nearly wept when he wiped it clean and read it aloud, precisely as it was printed:

> *Tu grass Hop Per digins 30 myle*
> *Kepe the Trale nex the bluffe.*

She bit at her lip, let her gaze wander across the enormous land. "Grass Hopper diggings? That's Grasshopper Creek, near Bannack, isn't it? Where Papa was headed."

Had he followed these crude instructions? And what had he found at the end of that thirty-mile trek? If he ever made it there at all, that is.

"Best move on," he said, "check it out."

She nodded and made a soft sound to the mare. The two had become so attuned to each other that no commands were ever necessary.

As they followed the trail to Bannack, Tressie took a look over her shoulder. Farther south in the Bitterroots someone named Majors waited, if they could believe what they'd learned. Maybe they shouldn't make this detour to Bannack.

"Do you think there's anything left of the town?"

"Hard to say," he replied. "I heard she's nearly deserted, that everyone fled to Alder Gulch when they struck color there, but who knows? Bannack was declared the temporary headquarters of the new territory of Montana so there was something there. But last December it moved to Virginia City, I hear."

She didn't say anything for a while. Before she could ask more about this wild new territory, the beauty of the majestic mountains struck her mute.

Nothing came of their trip to Bannack. It was, like Reed had thought, a sleepy little town on the verge of death and nobody there had ever heard of Evan Majors. It took another day to ride back out to the main trail and once again head south, this time toward Lima in the Bitterroots and yet another search. She prayed it, too, wouldn't be fruitless.

Occasionally they met up with travelers on the trail, some headed north, others south. None roused any suspicion and she began to believe that her earlier fears of being followed were just her imagination. Everywhere they went, everyone they talked to, listened patiently to their queries about Papa's whereabouts, then shook their heads. Had Evan Majors vanished off the face of the earth? It began to seem so.

On a peaceful, very hot afternoon, Reed said they had to be very near Lima. Hope grew once again in her heart. It was time this was over and done with. In her mind she practiced what she would say to Papa, how she would vent her hatred, make him sorry.

Despite her anxiety, her need to see this finished, Reed insisted they not push the horses but let them set their own pace. The words were no sooner out of his mouth when a great whooping and hollering echoed from the trail ahead. Rounding a bend, the couple spotted a gang of riders coming at them. Before they could meet up, however, the riders veered off the trail and headed through the woods.

Shouts of, "There's gonna be a hanging. A hanging," reached Tressie's ears and she stared wide-eyed at Reed.

Several wagons overflowing with people, including a few fancy women, emerged out of the cloud of dust left by the riders. They too made the turn into the woods.

Tressie and Reed waited there a moment, watching the crowd disappear from sight.

"Well," he finally said. "Looks like the whole town is here. Could be we might learn something, but it's up to you. A hanging isn't exactly a pretty sight."

She gulped down a knot of nausea. "How far are we from where Papa was supposed to be?"

That'd be Lima right up the road, I'd judge. Probably closest to his claim...if the man we heard tell of is your pa. You know we can't be sure of our information."

She shrugged and nudged the mare into the woodland trail. "And that's what we came here to find out. Reckon we'd better get to it."

As they walked their mounts, a rider came up on them from behind. A latecomer, and in a hurry. Reed hailed him.

"Who they hanging?"

"A Major something-or-other, I hear," the man shouted, and kept right on riding, whopping at his horse's butt with a wadded felt hat.

"Reed? Surely that couldn't be—"

"Stay here," he said. "Wait right here. I'll find out."

"I can't. Suppose it is him. You wouldn't know the difference. No, I'm going with you."

"Dammit. I can find out. You don't want to see this."

"If it's him I'll make them stop," she said, and quite abruptly nudged the mare with both heels. Not accustomed to such handling, the small horse laid back her ears and took off at a gallop. He could do nothing but spur his gelding on to keep up.

She tightened both knees, shifted her weight to the stirrups, and let the mare have her head.

Surely this wasn't Papa, for he'd never do anything that would get him hung. A wanderer he might be, but a lawbreaker? Never. There'd been some mistake. Still, she couldn't take the chance. Maybe it was another Majors. The name wasn't all that unusual. Some men even carried Major as a first name. Then there were majors in the Army. All sorts of possibilities occurred to her by the time she broke from the woods into a small clearing, Reed right on her heels. There she saw a sight that nearly stopped her heart.

Beneath a towering, gnarly old tree stood a circle of armed men, rifles at the ready. In their center the unlucky victim sat astride a bony horse, hands tied behind him, a noose around his neck. The man's head was tilted back so that he appeared to stare upward at the thick branch holding the rope.

All she could see was a crop of dusty brown hair and a disreputable old shirt. It could be Papa. Screaming "Noooo" in a long, drawn-out wail, she spurred the mare through the milling crowd, scattering the vigilantes.

Heads swiveled, including that of the unfortunate man about to be strung up. She caught a glimpse of a pale face, rolling eyes, a mouth opened wide, before his horse let out a disgusted snort and bolted. The noose tightened, jerking the rider out of his saddle. He swung back and forth in a wild arc, legs kicking frantically, his entire body jerking and twitching. Women screamed, men shouted.

Tressie leaped from her horse, her intention to grab the hanging man's feet, but the nearest vigilante outguessed her and tackled her around the waist. Both thumped to the ground in a great cloud of dust. Because of her clothing he thought she was a young man, so the rowdy treatment came as no surprise. It didn't make her any happier, though, and she kicked and screeched, clawing at the face of her attacker as they rolled around on the ground.

Rifle in one hand, Reed leaped from his galloping horse into the melee. He took a moment to make up his mind whether to rescue Tressie or try to save the man dangling at the end of the rope. He chose the unfortunate man, grabbing him by the legs. Maybe if the fall hadn't broken his neck, he could keep him from being strangled by the tight noose. But it was obvious as soon as he got a good hold that the man was dead weight. It was too late to do anything for him.

Reed let go and turned to Tressie, who sobbed in frustration because she couldn't break the ironclad hold of her captor. Waving the rifle around like a saber, he said, "Turn her loose now, mister."

A man in black holding a Bible whined, "Hell, I didn't even get to say the words. What kind of a hanging is this, anyway? Send a man on to his maker without the words."

"Shut up, Brother Dawson," a gangly fellow with a bobbing Adam's apple said. He then pointed his rifle at Tressie while two cohorts hauled her to her feet. "Now, just what the hell's this all about? We just might have us another hanging here if you don't explain yourself real good, young fella."

One of the men holding on to Tressie shouted, "Hank, disarm that other one 'fore he shoots someone." Then, turning to Tressie, he said, "Now, mister, you've got some explaining to do. You understand that you caused this here hanging, 'fore he was even ready to send the major here on. There was words needed saying. We was about to find out what he done with the goods he stole. Suppose you explain why you didn't want him to talk."

"Who was he? What was his name? I want to see," she cried, struggling to get free.

The man called Hank held his rifle on Reed, having disarmed him as ordered, and everyone stared at Tressie.

"Where's the sheriff?" Reed asked.

The one with the Adam's apple snorted. "Hell, we ain't got no sheriff around these parts. You break a law, we take care of it. No need for a sheriff. And you two is about fixing to taste of our law if you don't do some fast talking."

'You shouldn't have hung him without a trial," Tressie wailed, now convinced it was Papa swaying in the breeze.

"The major? Didn't need no trial, boy. The man robbed the general store, took a whole case of peaches plus some other stuff. Done it right under the nose of half the town, then shot the onliest two fellers with the guts to try and stop him. We run him down with a posse and brung him here to the hanging tree. Now if that ain't swift and fair justice, I don't know what is."

Hank agreed, "A trial's a flat waste of time. Now, what's your reason for trying to save his ornery hide?" He addressed the question at Reed and nudged him with the barrel of his rifle. "You in cahoots? You and this green un?"

"Now, hold it," Reed said. "We don't know a thing about a robbery. We're looking for a man name of Evan Majors, and we heard a feller named Majors was being hung. We just came along to see if they were one and the same, that's all."

Adam's apple grinned, showing a gap between crooked front teeth. "Why you looking for this Majors fella?"

Reed glanced at Tressie for help. She wiggled and kicked at the shins of her two captors.

"I'm his daughter," she yelled in frustration. "And if these two would let me go, I could tell right quick if that's him."

Henry widened his eyes, then twitched his head in her direction and the two men let her go. "Keep your eye on that one," he said toward Reed, and walked with Tressie to where the poor hanged man dangled. Sweeping off his hat in a belated gesture of respect for the dead, Henry gazed up into the purple, bloated face of the dead man. "Should a said you was a she," he muttered. Then, "That your pappy, ma'am?"

For a moment she couldn't force her gaze upward. Her heart thumped painfully in her throat and she felt dizzy. If it was Papa, she supposed she would faint. If it wasn't, she might faint anyway, because she'd never looked at a hanged body before. She wished Reed were beside her.

Ever so slowly she raised her eyes. Past the scuffed boots, toes turned inward toward each other, up over the ripped knees of the britches and a gray shirt that had once been white. Around the neck, the noose cut into the flesh and the head tilted unnaturally to one side. There was the mouth, tongue protruding, the nose with a thin trickle of blood running from one nostril, then the eyes, bulging and frantic. A widow's peak divided the long brown hair that hung in dirty strands around the dead face.

"It's not him," she whispered huskily. "Not him, not him."

Without warning, her knees folded under her and dark flashes obscured her vision so that the swaying body faded. Then, like a bolt of light from an overhanging black cloud, she realized that she had actually precipitated the hanging by riding through the crowd shouting at the top of her voice. Hadn't that man said so? She had hung this poor soul!

Throwing her hands over her face, she began to bawl quite loudly as if her heart were broken.

Reed, still held at gunpoint, took in the pitiful sight and, not having heard her earlier comment, thought the hanged man was indeed Evan Majors.

"Listen, you hunk of lard," he snarled at the one poking the rifle in his ribs, "you let me go take care of her, or I'll carve you up in little pieces and feed you to the crows." His knife appeared in one hand so quickly that Hank, an unfortunate vigilante who hadn't wanted any part in this hanging anyway, staggered backward, jabbering, "He's got a knife. The breed's got a knife."

Reed barreled his way through the surprised crowd to Tressie's side. By this time she had sunk to her knees in the dirt, continuing to cry. Hank, who hadn't yet caught on that she was a woman, stared in dismay at such an outburst from a young man.

Reed dropped to his knees, still holding the knife.

"Honey, I'm sorry. Dammit, I'm so sorry. But you'll be okay. It's over with, anyway." He gathered her in his arms and there they knelt, swaying back and forth gently, while high above, the killer and thief, a major and deserter from the Confederate Army who had never been any closer to the high plains than Fort Laramie, did a little swaying of his own.

Tressie struggled to explain to Reed that the man wasn't her father, but she felt so bereft at having caused the man's hanging, she could do nothing but babble.

The folks who had attended the ceremony meandered around awhile, not sure if they had been cheated of their afternoon's entertainment or if maybe the show they saw hadn't been even better. After a while, when it appeared that nothing else was going to happen, most of them wandered away, including Brother Dawson, who muttered his disappointment while cramming a tattered Bible into his saddlebag. Henry, who seemed to be in charge; Jake, the man with the Adam's apple; and Hank Norton, the bumbling fellow Reed had pulled a knife on, considered this entire thing unfinished, so stuck around to put things to rights.

The three vigilantes watched Reed and Tressie for a while, eyeing each other with disbelief. "No sense at all in two fellows acting like that," Hank finally said with disgust.

"One's a woman, fool. Reckon they had anything to do with the major's shenanigans?" Jake asked.

Hank Norton gaped. "Well, that breed pulled a knife on me. He would have scalped me, too, if I hadn't got away from him."

"That's a load of bull, Hank. You didn't get away. You was so scared you shook loose."

Henry and Jake laughed at poor Hank's expense.

All three turned in expectation when a wagon rattled into the clearing.

"It's Clete, come to claim the body," Henry said.

Jake gestured toward Reed and Tressie, who were still wrapped in each other's arms beneath the hanged man. "What do we do about them?"

Hank shrugged. "Aw, hell. One hanging a day's enough for me. Leave 'em be. You ask me, them two fellers got enough troubles as it is." He turned and waved at Clete as he went to his horse. Henry and Jake, discussing the downright plain stupidity of their friend Hank, stayed to cut down the body for the undertaker. Then they, too, left the clearing.

Reed was afraid he would never get Tressie settled down, but he really didn't mind holding her in his arms. He paid no attention as the undertaker's wagon clattered away, leaving him alone with her.

Awkwardly he rubbed at her head. "Shh, honey. Everything's going to be all right. Stop crying now, you'll be sick."

She hiccuped and said damply, "I killed him, I killed him."

"You did no such thing, darlin'. They hung him."

"But if I...if I hadn't...rode in...like...like I was...oh, Reed. I made them go ahead and hang him. Maybe he wouldn't...they might have changed their minds."

"That's nonsense, Pure and simple. Come on, now, dry your eyes and stop this. You didn't hang anyone, and most especially not Evan Majors. I'm sorry he's dead, but you didn't kill him."

"Oh, not Papa. That wasn't—I mean, the body—it wasn't Papa. Oh, goodness, no." She began to cry again, but softer and more controlled.

Not Majors? Confused, he hugged her some more, though his knees were getting mighty tired of kneeling in the rock-encrusted dirt under the hanging tree. What a day it had been, and now to learn that they still hadn't found Evan Majors, when he'd thought for sure…. He sighed. Would he never have this woman, or was he destined to trail around all over the West for the rest of his life searching for this man she both hated and loved? He wasn't sure he could take much more. Enough was enough.

"Come on, girl, get on your feet," he urged, and hauled her up with him. "We need to have us a talk, and I don't reckon this is a good place to do it, right here under a hanging tree. Let's find us a camp for the night, what do you say?"

Seeing the distressed look on his face, she tried to get hold of her emotions. "I'm sorry, it was just such a shock. First thinking we'd found him, then finding out it wasn't him at all, then thinking I'd hanged him. It was pretty upsetting."

"Oh, it was that, all right," he muttered, and went to fetch their horses, which were munching listlessly at green leaves on low-hanging branches nearby. He had a good hold on both bridles before it occurred to him how funny the entire situation had been, when you got right down to it.

And what had all those folks thought about him and Tressie busting up their pleasure and then carrying on so? Stories of the hanging of Major, whoever-the-hell-he-was, might grow into one of the most oft-repeated tales in these parts for years to come. He was chuckling when he returned to where Tressie waited.

Keeping a low profile, they rode through Lima and continued on another hour or so before camping on the edge of a stream far enough away from the main road so they couldn't be seen.

Reed still wasn't sure some of the vigilantes might not reconsider the day's events and decide to come after the two of them.

Before dark she waded upstream until she was completely out of sight of the camp. The creek curved away from an outcropping, and she wandered along a smaller stream. Breaking through a thick undergrowth of brush, she approached a cavelike shelter. A waterfall tumbled through a hole high above into a hollowed-out basin. The perfect place to bathe.

Stripping out of her clothes, she waded in up to her knees, leaving deep footprints in the smooth black sand along the water's edge. She eased down, submerging all but her head. Idly, she fingered through the sand, fisting up handfuls and washing them away just beneath the surface of the water.

The last rays of the setting sun penetrated the thick trees and fell across her hand momentarily flashing on something. She dug it out. Holding the rock up to catch the last of the evening's light, she gasped at the golden sheen. Surely it couldn't be gold. She turned the nugget, which was about the size of the end of her thumb, rubbed at it.

Then the sun was gone and she could no longer see much of anything in the isolated glen.

Heart beating high in her throat, she clutched the mysterious rock as she hastened into her britches and shirt. Without binding her breasts or even buttoning the shirt all the way, she ran back toward camp, carrying her shoes.

Reed had a fire going and she approached him as speechless as she'd ever been. She wanted to babble or shout or something, but nothing would come out of her mouth but a squawk.

Seeing her so frantic, he thought for a moment something was after her. A bear, maybe, or some crazed vigilante set on hanging them both. He grabbed up his rifle.

She panted to a halt in front of him and held out the nugget, eyes flashing in the light from the blazing fire.

Reed took it. "What is it, Tressie, girl? Cat get your tongue? What is this?"

She still couldn't say anything, just danced from one foot to the other and watched him.

He gave the nugget a closer look, put the rifle down, and

bent closer to the fire. "Where did you find this?" he asked, pulling out his knife to scrape at the surface.

She turned and pointed, looked back at him, finally croaked out, "Is it gold?"

He rubbed the nugget against his teeth, looked at it again, then nodded slowly as if in a trance. "Show me where you found it," he said softly. "Was there anyone else around? A camp or signs of a claim?"

"I don't know, I didn't look, but I didn't notice anyone."

Truth was, they hadn't seen signs of panning since before they took their inadvertent part in today's hanging. Gold fever hadn't yet made its way this deep into the mountains, or maybe no one had run across anything. Men tended to hunt where there was easier access. It was like the old story about the fishing hole. Find a good place to fish, even if you didn't catch anything.

He refused to believe she could have accidentally found a valuable gold deposit. Probably just the one nugget, something they could sell for a few months' expenses. But you never knew, and he had to see for himself.

"Take me there now," he told her.

Dropping her shoes, she headed back into the creek. 'You can't get there following either bank, it's too wild, you'll have to wade the water," she told him. "I was just taking a bath, sitting there playing in the sand, and there it was. It's back in a cavelike place under a waterfall."

Reed's own heart pounded. Gold was often washed down from higher in the mountains. Beneath a waterfall was a perfect place to find nuggets like this. Still…

"What color was the sand?" he asked, feeling as if his tongue overflowed his mouth.

"The prettiest black you ever saw," she said. "Here, in here. She led them along the creek. I almost missed it in the dark. You don't suppose there's snakes in here, do you?"

"Snakes?" he asked incredulously. "Snakes? You have found a gold nugget the size of your thumb and you're worried about snakes. Good Lord. Do you realize we might be rich?"

"Oh, do you think so? Truly?" She wasn't sure how she felt about that. If they had to stake a claim and work it, then she would probably never find Papa. They wouldn't even look anymore, and his fate would be lost forever.

By the time they reached the waterfall it was so dark neither could see anything. They stumbled around in there for a while, then gave up.

"We'll come back first thing in the morning and take a good look," he said finally. "It's been here all this time, it ain't going anywhere. Oh, Lord, Tressie," he shouted, and pulled her close.

She nestled into his arms, trembling a bit in the knee-deep water. The warmth of his body washed over her and she hugged him tight. He lowered his head and she raised her face, finding his seeking lips in the pitch-black. Her arms snaked around his neck and he wrapped her up in a strong hug, shuddering a bit himself.

In the summer darkness, frogs and crickets, night creatures of all kinds, filled the air with their song. At that moment, when they were eerily suspended in a darkness that shut out time, she decided that she wanted nothing but this man, holding her close, protecting and loving her for the rest of her life. Nothing frightened her when he held her like this, and when he pulled away it was as if she had lost her natural hold on things.

Why then couldn't she just put her hate and need for revenge behind her? Give everything to Reed Bannon, and take everything he offered in return.

"Ah, Tressie, I do love you so," he whispered. "Let's get back to camp."

Holding hands, they made their careful way along the creek, and it took a long while before they spotted the campfire, burned down some but still glowing like a guiding star in the depths of the wilderness.

As they approached the camp, paying more attention to each other than to their surroundings, a twig snapped and gravel scattered near the camp. He froze and pulled her behind him. He had left both the rifle and his knife in camp with his saddlebags. They had made plenty of noise as they approached, and an intruder in their camp couldn't have helped but hear them coming.

"Get down on your knees in the brush there," he whispered. "Don't move, don't come out for anything. You understand?"

Throat locked tightly, she nodded vigorously and obeyed.

Reed crouched down and made his way around the edge of the clearing, out of the glow of firelight. Pausing behind the trunk of a large tree, he stared at their campsite until his eyes ached. Nothing moved. The horses were hobbled at his back, not where the noise had come from.

Someone had been snooping around, but whoever it was appeared to have lit out when he and Tressie returned.

What in the hell was going on? Why would anyone be snooping around their camp? They didn't have anything worth stealing, unless it was Indians wanting the horses. Or maybe Henry or Jake had second thoughts and decided to check them out further. That was surely it. But why didn't they just do it openly?

After waiting a few more minutes, he called out to her that everything was all right. She approached the firelight cautiously. "Who was it?"

"I don't know. I didn't see anyone, and nothing has been disturbed. The rifle's right where I left it; so is everything else."

By this time he had convinced himself that his ears had played tricks on him, and one of the animals had simply moved around, making him think someone was prowling on the other side of the camp.

"What was it you wanted to talk to me about?" she asked, settling down close to the fire to get warm.

"What?" he asked absentmindedly.

"You said we had to talk, back there after the…after the hanging. What about?"

"Oh, that," he said. He thought of the nugget and what it could mean, of how he felt holding her. The discussion about stopping this insane search for Evan Majors could wait until they checked out her discovery. If they decided to file a claim and pan some gold here, it would be settled for a while anyway.

He really dreaded telling her that he had no desire to keep traipsing around the country after a man who obviously didn't want to be found anyway.

She sidled around the fire and snuggled up against him. "Then let's sleep together tonight. I don't want to sleep alone."

He put his arm around her, pulled her head to his shoulder. Sometimes a man just couldn't fight anymore. The darkness around them seemed not so harmless as he wished. Something or someone lurked out there. He felt that as he'd never felt anything before. Who or what it was, he had no idea.

"I don't feel like sleeping alone, either," he said, pulling her up into his lap. He slipped one hand inside the front of her partially buttoned shirt and caressed her breast.

She gave herself to him slowly, their love as sweet and warm as a summer night.

Nine

Hidden in the secret darkness of the woods, he ran clumsy fingers over the beaded leather bag. He could almost taste victory sweetening the bitter hate he'd carried like a loathsome burden.

It wouldn't be long now. The first time the breed left the woman alone, well, that would be too bad for her. He would steal her just as Race had stolen Bright Fox. And kill her the same, too. Well, nearly the same. It would do Reed no good to deny he was Race Brannigan's whelp. Changing his name didn't make it so. He would pay for what he and his daddy had done. Pay good for the rest of his miserable life.

The big man settled quietly against the trunk of a tree, keeping his eye on the couple lying beside the campfire. Like a cat over a rat hole, he had them now, and there was time to play.

Anxious to take a good look at the place where Tressie had found the gold nugget, Reed dragged her out of the mound of blankets at first light. He didn't even want to stop for breakfast.

"Later, we can eat later," he told her, grabbing her hand and heading for the stream as soon as she was dressed.

"Slow down. You'd think you were a gold-hungry prospector, the way you're acting."

He only laughed. But it was true that he saw in the gold find a possibility of being with the woman he loved for the rest of his life. No more running from ghosts, no more seeking what wasn't there to be found—her runaway pa, Reed's misplaced pride. They could have a home and family someplace out West. Maybe California.

"In there," she cried, hauling him up short.

Together they pushed through the brush, following the trickling stream of water that flowed into the main branch. At last they emerged into a small clearing fronting an overhanging bluff. She pointed at the falls tumbling through a hole in the slab of rock at least twenty feet above their heads.

He gaped at the secluded glen. "How in the world did you find this, girl?"

She shrugged. "I don't know. I wanted a good place to take a bath in private, so I just kept looking. Come on."

Together they waded into the indigo pool of water. Her footprints from the evening before were still visible in the black sand on the bank.

She squatted and ran her fingers through the grit. "I just dug up a handful and sifted it, like this," she said, and did so. Another nugget peeked out, smaller than the first, but quite impressive. "My goodness, look!"

He laughed sharply and jerked his head all around, thinking that surely something couldn't be right about plucking nuggets up as if they were common stones. Then he filled his own fists and, opening both hands beneath the surface, let the black sand drift from his palms. In the crystalline water, flakes of gold floated toward the bottom like glittering rain.

"Good Lord," he said prayerfully. He glanced all around again. He expected at any moment for someone to leap out and shoot them for trespassing on their claim. But there were no signs anywhere that a human had ever been near this place. He'd been in this country long enough to know a claim such as this would be marked and well protected.

As if mesmerized, she stared at the two nuggets she now held. "What do we do? Good heavens, what do we do?"

"Stake our claim, now. Ride into Lima and register it, then come back out here and start panning, my girl."

"But Reed, you don't just go out one night to take a bath and end up finding gold. Not like this."

"Well, this time I reckon you do, darlin'."

He pondered on that for a bit, then leaped high into the air, tossed his hat, and whooped. Droplets of multi-hued water arced in a rainbow around him. Coming down with a tremendous splash, he reached for Tressie and pulled her into a hug. "Someone has to be first, and I reckon this time it's us."

Clutching the nuggets in one hand, she raised her gaze to meet his. His shaggy black hair, wetly plastered around the harshly chiseled face, the depth of his eyes soft as a velvet night, the joy that transformed his somber features, all made her forget everything that had gone before in her life. What this discovery would mean to their lives she had no idea, but seeing him so happy filled her own heart with a joy as warm and sweet as summer honey.

She cupped one side of his face in her palm and tilted his mouth down to hers.

"Oh, girl. Sweet girl," he said. "None of this is worth a thing if I don't have you." He'd let it all go, in a minute. If only he could keep her this way always.

She tasted the fire of his passion, his need for her, and ran her tongue around the soft inner flesh of his mouth. His manner allowed such trust. No rough, hurtful play with this man. In his tender embrace it was easy to push memories of Papa's betrayal aside. It was even easy to say it didn't matter, that she didn't care if she ever found him. Until, that is, one came awake in the wee dark hours of morning haunted by memories.

You didn't forget a cruelty, a vow for revenge made over a grave, no matter your excuse.

Reluctantly they parted.

He licked her tangy taste from his lips and gazed down into her dazzling green eyes. "I guess we'd better get to business, huh?"

Beneath his grin she caught a glimpse of troubled sorrow. Before she could explore its meaning, he turned away. They set to work marking the outer perimeter of their claim by stacking a series of rocks in each of four corners.

"Now what?" she asked when they had finished.

"I've never done this before, but I'd guess we'll have to pace it off, see how far it is from the creek and the main trail."

"Who goes to town and who stays here?" she asked.

"Considering our last confrontation with folks from Lima, I'd guess that to be the most dangerous of the two jobs, so I'll do it. But I think we have to have something to show, so I'll take the gold to the assayer and he'll tell us what to do next."

Tressie giggled. "I'll bet come tomorrow morning there'll be men panning this creek just like they were at Alder Gulch when we passed there."

"Word of gold does get around."

They waded out to their campsite hand in hand. 'You know," Tressie said, "Papa might hear about this. Wouldn't that be something if our strike made him come to us?"

"Dammit, can't you forget your hate for two minutes at a time?" He was immediately sorry for his outburst, but her words had successfully shattered the plans he was making for their future. He had struck out in defense of his very life.

She stopped in the middle of the creek. "Well, no, I can't. He killed my mama, and abandoned me and the little one, and so it's a little hard to just make his memory disappear forever."

"It seems he did a pretty good job of that himself, without your help," he said.

She watched him stride out of the water and into camp. No matter what happened, even uncovering gold nuggets that would choke a mule, she and Reed seemed destined to fight over her mission. She chased after him. "If that's the way you feel, why don't you just stay here with your precious gold and I'll go on looking for him by myself."

"Don't be dumb. You wouldn't last a week out there alone."

"Oh, yeah. Well, that's just what you think. I was taking care of myself when you found me, and I can just go on doing it. I don't need any old gold to make me happy. You can just keep it all."

'You try to leave, I'll hog-tie you, girl," he said softly. "I mean it, I will. I ain't letting you loose out here in this godforsaken land all alone, and I don't care what you think."

'You wouldn't dare," She faced him trembling with rage. "Oh, yes I would dare, and it would be for your own good."

"Well, we'll just see about that." She whirled and started tossing her belongings haphazardly in a pile on one of the blankets where they'd slept together the previous night. Speechless, he watched her fold, roll, and tie the blanket. She hefted her saddle, but found she couldn't carry both, so dropped the roll and headed for the mare who grazed nearby. Water squished in her clothes as she walked.

'Tressie," he commanded, chasing after her. The mare eyed them both with rolling eyes and backed away.

Gritting her teeth, she shushed the frightened animal and tossed the saddle on its back. Anger masked her reasoning. Fear that he would let her go almost made her sick, yet she could see no way to back down now.

'You know I won't…can't let you do this," he warned in that steady, soft voice of his.

"Then don't," she thought she said aloud and went right on working with the cinch.

"You didn't put her blanket on," he said.

She thought she would choke with the anguish that instantly overpowered her. She whirled, doubled up her fists, and began to cry. "Why did I ever have to meet you? Why didn't I die there with Mama? How could he do that to us? I hate him, hate him, hate him, and I want to tell him so. I wish he was dead. Do you hear me? I wish he was dead, dead, dead."

He took two steps and caught her in his arms. She remained stiff and unyielding, shaking with pent-up fury.

Even though she didn't respond to him, he hung on to her rigid body. 'You don't mean that, darlin'. None of it. Just quieten down, now. You've got to forgive yourself, do you hear me? You can't go on blaming yourself for all that happened. Girl, listen to me, would you?"

"No, no. It wasn't my fault, it wasn't."

"I know that, but you don't. That's why you just keep up this crazy fighting with yourself. Let it go now, you hear me? Let it go so you can live. So we can live."

Her legs weakened. "I don't think I can," she whimpered.

Filled with compassion, he lifted her, curled one arm under her knees, and carried her back to where they had slept together. He figured if he didn't give in, he'd win this tough woman/child one day. She sure did set high standards for herself, standards no human could ever live up to. If they didn't settle this question of Evan Majors's whereabouts, she never would be able to live with herself.

If he ever got his hands on the man, he'd shake him so hard his eyeballs fell out in the dust, then he'd make him tell Tressie how sorry he was for the wicked thing he'd done. Then he'd kick him all the way up to the divide and off the other side.

She lay where he placed her, watching him with moist eyes.

He kissed the corner of her mouth and experimented with a teasing tone. "Do I have to tie you up now?"

She rolled her head back and forth. "You wouldn't anyway."

"No, I wouldn't anyway, but dammit, you sure did give me a scare. I was thinking I was going to have to do something. You're your own worst enemy, girl, I'll swear if you ain't. Could be you left home too wet."

She giggled weakly. "What an awful thing to say."

"Well, sometimes I think you still need someone to tell you what to do."

"You said no one can make us do things, that we do what we want."

"Oh, sure, throw that back at me. You know exactly what I meant. Whatever we do, and that includes your ill-begotten papa, is our own fault. We can't go laying it off on other folks, blaming them for our own weaknesses. One of these days you'll understand that he did what he did and has to take responsibility. It wasn't your fault."

"Oh, I understand it," she said primly. "Anyway, what makes you so almighty smart?"

He rubbed at her jaw with the ball of his thumb. "Oh, I'm not so smart. I've done plenty of dumb things. Things I wish to hell I could take back. And I have to live with them. I wish I deserved your love, Tressie. Truly I do."

"But you do, you do."

He looked away, staring out across the creek. "Well, maybe someday I will. Now let's get busy. We need to move the camp closer to our claim and get down to some serious panning."

She sat up, throwing off the earlier distress.

They spent the rest of the morning moving camp, actually managing to joke with each other as they worked. Using a small hatchet, he cleared saplings from the forest floor near where the stream flowed from under the overhang. There wasn't room beneath the bluff for the animals, a campfire, and sleeping arrangements, so they hobbled the mule and both horses across the main stream in a small field of lush grass.

When he returned from stepping off the claim they would file, she had dinner cooked: fried fatback in dandelion greens with johnnycake alongside. They divided the meal, and he dug in, smacking his lips.

She enjoyed watching him eat. "After we finish I'm putting some beans on to cook. We'll be here awhile. I can start fixing decent meals for you."

"This is pretty decent," he said. "1 was starving for fresh greens. Wouldn't a little vinegar be good on them?"

"Put it on your list," Tressie said, and took another bite.

He glanced up quickly. "List?"

"For when you go to town to file our claim. That gold is surely worth enough to buy us some vittles."

He grinned at her with a silly look on his face. He'd forgotten they were rich. "Yeah, I expect you're right. Oh, and, I know we're all alone out here, but maybe you ought to do something about..." He gestured with his spoon at her chest.

The flannel shirt she wore was unbuttoned halfway down, revealing much of the lush pale beauty of her breasts. There was little left to the imagination. Flashing her eyes mischievously at him, she fingered two more buttons loose.

"Aw, hell, girl, don't do that."

Carefully placing her empty plate on a rock near the fire, she rose in a sensuous movement, at the same time releasing the button at her waist. The baggy pants slid down her long, lean legs to bunch around trim ankles.

"Tressie," he warned, poking a last bite of johnnycake in his mouth and rising. "We've got work to do."

The shirt, all that covered her body, came off in one slick motion of her arms. She stood there before him, the opulent jade forest at her back, the music of the waterfall playing around her. Sunlight danced with shadows over her erect breasts and flashed in her auburn tresses.

"Reed," she said softly. "Come here or I'm coming after you." She trailed a finger between her breasts and down past her belly button.

"You little savage," he groaned, and took off his shirt slowly, matching her eroticism with some of his own. When he stood naked before her, still not making a move in her direction, she cupped both hands under her breasts and lifted them, twitching the nipples with both thumbs.

He swayed and held his ground, gazing at her from half-closed eyes. A craving of such intensity invaded her that she was nearly knocked to her knees. She staggered a bit, saw him through a haze as if only imagining his presence. It was hard to tell where the sheen from his bronze body became rays of woodland light. Hands hanging loosely at his sides, he shifted his weight, cocking one lean hip. A breeze lifted his long black hair. He was like something from an erotic dream. Beyond his appearance, he possessed an inner radiance and kindness of spirit that made him very special.

When she could no longer stand being parted from him, she lifted one arm and bade him come to her. He did, taking her hand while running the other over her body. Gooseflesh followed the journey of his fingertips across one breast, down the curve of her tiny waist, and into the downy mound between her legs.

Dropping to his knees, he placed his warm lips against her flesh, flicking out his tongue as he moved ever so slowly downward. She arched her head backward and cried out while his tongue performed maddening pirouettes deep within her.

When her legs would no longer support her, she slithered down the length of him, until they knelt body to body. He smelled of musk and the leather of their saddles, and a wild unnameable fragrance that triggered an overpowering passion in her. His moist flesh embraced every inch of hers as they lay back in the cool green moss.

When he lifted her body against his, they slipped gently into the shallow water. The quivering waves washed between them, lapping, lapping, licking away their juices.

He poised on the very edge of an ecstasy so supreme as not to be bearable. He would kill for this woman. He would die for her. These things he knew with a certainty he had never before experienced. He would do anything to see that she was happy. Even leave her, if that's what it took, for he had never felt so totally one with another being on this earth. She dwelled in his soul and she would forever be there, even if he never saw her again. But he would do anything to keep her with him.

He dreamed that night of the running. Running from his mother's people and their primitive rites of passage, running from the war and that all-too-savage rite peculiar to the white man, and worst of all running always from himself and what he feared dwelled in his innermost recesses that made of him a coward.

He awoke drenched in sweat, panting and reaching out for her, fearful that she had somehow followed him into that terrible dream world and seen what he truly was.

In her sleep she made a soft sound and snuggled into his grasping arms, tucking her head against his chest. He feared the day he would have to tell her his dark coward's secret. It was a long time before he went back to sleep again.

The next morning he saddled up his gelding, stuffed into the front pocket of his pants the drawstring pouch filled with gold they had found the day before, and kissed her.

"I'm leaving the rifle with you," he told her. "I'll be back as soon as I can."

She clung to his hand a moment, then put it to her lips in a farewell. "I'll be okay. You just be careful or you'll end up in jail, after what we did to their hanging."

His dark eyes glittered. "We? I was only an innocent bystander." Seeing her glowering look, he continued, "Ah, don't you worry, they'll be cooled down by now. Besides, we're a long way from the Army and the law. I'll be fine."

"You've got the list of supplies?"

He nodded, patted his shirt pocket. "I love you, girl. Now, don't worry."

"No, no, I won't." She backed away as he mounted, remained there watching him leave until the horse had crossed the creek and plodded through their earlier campsite toward the road to town.

With a sigh she leaped playfully through the water and back toward the gold claim. She had decided to pan for more gold during the hottest part of the afternoon, then go searching for edible plants in the cool of the evening. She didn't know much about roots and herbs in these mountains, but if she were back home in the Ozarks there would be a harvest of fruit ripe by now. Blackberries hanging in thick clusters on their wickedly thorned bushes, huckleberries that grew low on spindly plants, and the sweet, ground-hugging dewberries. She recalled the tart red plums she and Bitter Leaf had so enjoyed last summer. Maybe she could find some of those, too. First, though, she would put beans on to cook.

All caught up in readying the hot coals, placing the pot of water just so, and looking over the dried beans, handful at a time, she didn't hear the man enter the clearing. He came up on her so quiet she had no idea he was there until his massive arm locked around her from behind. The cloth sack tipped, spilling beans around on the ground. He lifted her completely off her feet, squeezing so hard she gasped for air. In her ear his hot, fetid breath whistled harshly.

"Behave, girlie, or I'll break your back, and I can do

it, too." He exerted more pressure to convince her and she crumpled over his arm.

When she came to, very little time must have passed, for he was carrying her in the same position, headed for the small pasture where her mare and the mule were grazing. She shoved and clawed at his hairy forearm, kicking out with bare heels. He just laughed at her, a huge booming sound that echoed off the bluffs and peaks.

"What do you want? Let me go. Are you crazy?" These questions she blurted out between painful gasps for air.

She feared passing out again. Had he come to steal the claim, take away their gold? Or worse, to kill her?

He made no reply, just grunted and shifted her around so that she could no longer kick him.

He tucked her under his arm like a sack of feed, her head faced forward and her legs stuck out behind. She looked down at his massive feet, encased in deerskin boots wet from wading the creek. His smell was that of rancid fat.

"Stop it!" she cried. "Who are you? Leave me alone!"

With amazement, she spotted her saddled mare and alongside waited a leggy black that must belong to this man. When and how had he done that? He had to have saddled the mare while Reed was still in camp, for there hadn't been time since he rode out.

My God, was this the man who had been following them? The one she had sensed but could never see?

He tossed her into the saddle so roughly that one thigh struck the horn painfully. "Straddle her. Do I have to tie your legs together, or are you going to behave?"

Later she realized that if she'd had better sense, she would have suffered less, but she lashed out, never having been wise when it came to controlling her mouth. "Behave? I'll hit you over the head with a rock first chance I get."

So, of course, he bound one ankle, drew the rawhide under the mare's belly and bound the other. Then he tied her wrists to the saddle horn. Drawing the thong tight so that she cried out, he said, "There, now, that'll keep you."

It was at that moment, when he stood at her mount's shoulder looking squarely up at her, that she recognized the man. And this time it wasn't her imagination, like with Dr. Gideon. Or all the other fleeting times when she'd thought she saw someone familiar who reminded her of this monstrous man. This was Dooley Kling, who was just like Papa. A man who would desert his wife and child without a backward glance. But what was he doing here, and what did he want with her?

"You…you filthy killer," she spat.

"Hush, girlie, or you'll wear a gag, too, and it'll be as tight as this gawdamn thong. You understand?"

Eyes filling and fear boiling from down deep in her stomach, she nodded so hard her teeth clacked together. He hadn't come for the gold claim but for her. But why? And what did he intend to do with her?

After he had her trussed, Kling went back to the camp on foot and she watched with puzzlement while he scratched in the dirt with a long stick. As she watched, Kling kicked over the pan of water and scattered the dry beans all around. He wanted Reed to know that something bad had happened to her. She wondered why, but didn't ask when he came back, for fear he would do as promised and gag her.

They rode the main trail, but not for long, for he soon cut off to the right and headed up what appeared to be nothing more than a goat trail. They were fast headed into high country. In front of them, snow-covered peaks cut jagged lines against the blue sky. It was dry season up there, but soon torrential rains would begin, rains that before long would turn to ice and snow.

She feared she wouldn't live to see it unless Reed could

somehow track them. He was good at that, like he was good at a lot of other things on the trail. And oddly enough, Kling made no effort to hide the signs of their passage.

They stopped the first night in a small meadow filled with white daisies surrounding a mirror-still lake. On the fringes of the forest golden aspen chattered in the breeze. The wind that touched her skin carried a misty tang from the high snows.

Kling unlashed one ankle and her wrists, then shoved her out of the saddle. With an outraged cry she tumbled to the ground in a heap. For a long while she lay in the brittle grass and rubbed at her tingling legs. When she could finally move them, she struggled to stand. It took all the effort she could muster. They had been riding almost all day without a break, though he had given her water twice.

"I have to go," she said thickly.

"You ain't going anywhere."

"No, I mean, I need to…please don't make me wet myself."

He studied her through squinted eyes, then finally nodded. "Do it there, where I can watch."

"No, please," she cried.

"Do it or forget it," he said, but did finally turn his back when she unfastened her britches and stood there glaring at him.

After hobbling the horses, he built a fire and boiled some coffee. He threw her a hard chunk of bread to go with the mud-black brew, and she swallowed both gratefully. She had to stay alive, any way she could, because as careless as this man was, Reed would catch them in no time.

She tried to imagine Reed's return to camp, his complete and utter distress at finding her and the mare gone. Would he ride out immediately or wait until morning? During the long, endless night, huddled without a blanket on the hard ground, she pictured, over and over, Reed setting out to rescue her. She had to survive for when he caught up to them.

⊛

At the general store in Lima, where the stagecoach delivered mail, Reed presented his list for supplies. The dark-haired, bespectacled storekeeper was friendly and nosy. Reed had about decided that out here on the frontier the two went together.

"You staying around these parts?" the man asked, fetching the first item off the list: two cans of peaches. Reed grinned widely. He hadn't read Tressie's list, and was pleased that she remembered what high stock he put in the syrupy golden fruit.

"Staking a claim down south."

The man raised brown eyes, widened them. "A claim? Gold? Say, ain't you the fellow who come to the hanging? You and that other fellow what turned out to be a girl raised such a ruckus?"

Reed glanced around the store. An old man sat in a straight chair, head nodding as if asleep, and a young man about Tressie's age pawed through some overalls.

"Yep, I reckon that was me and my, uh, my partner."

"Partnered with a girl and you're gonna pan for gold, are you?" The man snorted to show what he thought of such and pointed a narrow finger at the list. "Is this bacon? If so, I ain't got none."

Reed twisted to read the scrawl. "Looks like bacon, but you can put in fatback instead."

The storekeep nodded. "That I got." He went to a large wooden barrel and dug around in an assortment of salted meats till he came up with a chunk of pork fat. "You fellers' names?"

"What?" Reed said, staring through the window at a rider in the street. He rode stiffly erect, one hand on his thigh as if he'd been in the cavalry. That made Reed unaccountably nervous.

"Names. What names do you two go by?

"Oh." Reed thought about using a fake name, but couldn't think of one. Besides, like he'd told Tressie, they were a long way from the Army and the long arm of the law. "Reed Bannon's my name, and—"

"Bannon. Why, ain't that a crazy coincidence?"

Reed felt the hair on the back of his neck prickle. So they did know him after all. Would this man draw a hog-leg pistol out from under the counter and hold him for the vigilantes?

The man did go under the counter, but it was to pull out a stack of envelopes. "A letter come here for you just last week. Says General Delivery, Lima, Territory of Montana. Used to be Idaho, you know. Plumb strange how them government fellas keep a changing the names of places. One week I live in Oregon, the next Idaho, now it's Montana."

Reed chuckled at the little joke, overdoing it somewhat in his relief that he wasn't going to be the next man strung up to the hanging tree outside of town. He reached for the letter, wondering what in the world it could be. The only person who had any idea where they were headed was the pretty blond lady friend of Tressie's who owned the saloon in Virginia City. The letter Tressie had sent by stagecoach when they turned south must have made it to the Golden Sun Saloon after all.

Though anxious to read this letter he now clutched, Reed stuffed it into his shirt pocket. It might be addressed to him, but that was just because of the situation, and he knew it was really for Tressie. He'd let her read it aloud for the both of them when he got back to camp.

Meanwhile, he had to get to the assayer's.

"Say," he said to the storekeeper, who continued to lay out items from the list, "would you mind finishing that out while I go to the assayer's?"

Despite several references to the interrupted hanging of Major whatever-his-name-was, by midafternoon Reed had completed his business in Lima. He rode back into camp with the mysterious letter burning a hole in his pocket.

He had unsaddled his gelding and toted the two sacks of supplies into their new camp alongside the gold claim before it dawned on him that Tressie's mare was missing.

That's when he saw the mess someone had made in camp and found the message scratched in the dirt nearby.

Ten

At first Reed couldn't make out what was scrawled in the dirt. He saw the scattered beans, the overturned pot. Even then, for a split second longer, he considered that she had simply gone somewhere on her own. It didn't work.

An intense fear for her nearly blinded him. For a long while he just stood there staring down, not fully comprehending much of anything but that he had lost her. He had left her alone and unprotected and lost her. Coming back to his senses, he dropped the supplies and fell to both knees, tracing the gouges in the dirt with trembling fingers, race. Race? What kind of race?

It wasn't until he spotted the beaded deerskin bag that the name of his hated father slammed at him like a thrown rock. Race Brannigan. How he'd hope never to be forced to think of the name again.

He snatched up the bag, inspected it thoroughly. Yes, there it was, the peculiar symbol worked into the beading in the lower right-hand corner. This was the bag his grandmother had given him so long ago, the one Dooley Kling stole when he lit out and abandoned his newborn child.

But what could Dooley Kling and Reed's father possibly have to do with this? Father and son wouldn't know each other if they met face-to-face in broad daylight. Reed didn't know how or why, but Dooley Kling had been here and had left this cryptic message. And it was somehow connected to Reed's past. To his own father and mother.

His first impulse was to mount up and ride out, tracking that bastard Dooley Kling so he could catch him and rip him limb from limb. But if he was to save the woman he loved, he had to think, plan, listen to his head, not his heart. The man would not have left the message and the bag had he not wanted Reed to follow. So the trapper would leave plenty of sign, and he would keep an eye on his back trail. Reed would have to go very carefully.

He squinted into the sky. Maybe four hours of daylight left. Pushing, he could cover a lot of trail before dark.

He packed little food, keeping down the weight. Why hadn't he bought ammo at the general store this morning? He counted twenty-five rounds on hand. It would have to be enough. He didn't plan on getting in a shootout with Kling, not with Tressie in the way. All he needed now was water, a bedroll, and a mackinaw. Those tied to the saddle, he mounted up.

The letter in his shirt pocket was forgotten until dark caught up with him and he could no longer track his prey. By then he had followed them off the main trail. And he'd been right about the old bastard. Kling was making sure to leave plenty of sign to follow.

As he dismounted, he scowled toward the west, where the purpling peaks jagged against the silvering sky. Along the crest, lingering daylight sparkled on ice and snow, then faded. He shivered.

She was up there somewhere, and if Kling hurt her, he'd kill him. Slow and easy. The thought surprised Reed, for he'd never deliberately considered killing anyone before, not even during the war when he was firing at the unseen enemy. Shooting off a gun at someone because he threatened you was not the same as setting out to kill Dooley Kling. But dammit, the man had Tressie, and God only knew what hell she was going through. He tried not to think of that, or of the possibility of losing her. It might drive him crazy.

Boldly he built a campfire for the night. Let the son of a bitch know he was coming.

Besides, he needed light so he could read the letter.

Rose Langue wrote how only recently it had reached her ears that Evan Majors had been killed in a mining accident several months earlier. She told in great detail about how she had learned of Evan's death from the prospector who tried to use Tressie's tintype as an ante for a poker game at the Busted Mule.

Rose apologized for the delay in getting the word to Reed and Tressie and hoped they were faring well. And then she added some stuff about Lincolnshire that Reed scarcely scanned. He hadn't taken to the lanky Englishman and didn't care about what the man was up to.

Rose ended her letter with a request to stop by and see her the next time they were in Virginia City. The letter was dated August 7, a full month previously.

He held the two wispy sheets of paper between his fingers and stared into the fire, for a moment emptied of all feeling. Orange flame darted in a burst of wind that riffled the letter's pages. Slowly he creased the paper and inserted it with great care back into the envelope he had slit open with his knife. Then he dragged over his saddlebags and placed the letter inside. He wanted to keep it safe so he could show it to Tressie.

Dammit, if only they'd had the news a month ago, they might not have been here now.

Head in one hand, he massaged both temples with thumb and fingers. Tears pooled in his eyes and ran down his cheeks like trails of fire, and he wiped them ferociously away. Now that they were free, he and Tressie, to build a life, this bastard Kling had come along. And somehow it was all tied up with Race Brannigan, the father he had always despised for abandoning him. What a hell of a legacy the old man had left.

Before dawn erased the glittering stars, he was on the trail again, following tracks left by the two horses that carried Kling and Tressie.

A streak of sunlight burned across Tressie's cheek, awakening her from an exhausted sleep.

For a tense moment she lay very still. Where was he, and what was he doing? She heard only joyful bird song. Straightening her stiff legs, she cocked an ear and listened harder.

Despite the sun, she still felt cold and numb from spending the chilly night on the ground. Struggling to sit, she cried out with pain. He'd left her arms tied behind her back, and the thongs cut into her tender skin. Still, there was no sign he was in camp. Maybe the man had changed his mind and simply ridden away, leaving her there for Reed to find.

She rocked forward, backward, and was finally able to move to a position where she could see their camp. Her gaze drifted over Kling's saddle, the pile of blankets where he'd slept, the coffeepot steaming in the coals of last night's fire. So he was still around somewhere. But where?

And what did he have in mind for her today? Was Reed this very moment on their trail?

The aroma from the simmering pot was nearly unbearable. Her throat was so dry she could scarcely swallow and her empty stomach roiled with the harsh pangs of hunger. Her entire body ached and itched, her eyes burned, and her bladder was about to burst.

Other than that, I'm okay. She chuckled bitterly. At least she hadn't lost her sense of humor.

Licking at cracked lips, she scooted around until she had a full view of the meadow. Bitterroot bloomed among the daisies, each plant's singular roselike flower opening its lovely face to the sun. She thought of digging the fleshy root and cooking it up, smelling the pleasing fragrance not unlike sweet tobacco. The idea flooded her mouth with saliva.

"Well, I see you're awake," boomed Kling, and she jerked to rigid attention. The man was as quiet on his feet as Reed.

"I need to go to the toilet," she said.

"Is that all you do, girl, is pee?"

She shrugged and he loosened the rawhide around her ankles, half dragging her away from their camp. Pinpricks of pain darted up and down her numb legs, and she swayed to and fro.

"I can't till you untie my arms." If he wanted to humiliate her, he was doing a good job of it. He yanked the lashing off, and the pain was so intense she saw stars.

"And don't you run, either," he spat. "I'm a-fixing coffee, and if you run that'll mean I'll have to leave it to haul you back. That'll plumb rile me." He stomped away, sparing her no further glances.

Before returning willingly to Kling's custody, she briefly considered her chances if she made a run for it. She could hide out in the woods; he might not find her. But of course he would. There was very little undergrowth and the man was as cunning and single-minded as an animal. Besides, Reed would catch them before the day was out. There was no getting around that. And if she ran off into the wilderness, he might never find her, nor she him.

Back at the campsite, Kling seemed inclined to talk, bragging about how clever he'd been following them all these months. "Ever since you lit out from Virginia City," he crowed. "Seen everthing you did, too." His eyes glittered at her over a steaming tin cup of coffee. "Maybe you'll give me some of what you give him."

"Shut your filthy mouth!"

"Makes me no never mind. I get ready, I'll just take it. Appears to me you like it just fine."

She wanted to crawl out of hearing of the dirty sneering words. It didn't matter what he thought of her; just the same, the judgment embarrassed her. To think of this pig actually watching her and Reed make love sickened her. "You're lying. You didn't see anything."

"Well, how else would I know?" Hoarse laughter spurted from his mouth, startling the horses. They whinnied and tossed their heads, their hooves clinking in the rocky soil.

"Why are you doing this?" she asked.

"Ask your high-and-mighty fella." More laughter. "That is, if you get a chance."

"Oh, I'll get a chance, all right. He'll kill you."

Kling regarded her until she began to fidget. Then he tossed the dregs of coffee into the fire and rose, stretching trunklike arms high into the sky. "Time we was on our way, don't you think?"

He hadn't given her any coffee, but he did offer her the water canteen before breaking camp. She drank slowly and deeply, noticing with interest that he made no effort to cover the campfire or remove signs they had been there.

She prayed he wouldn't tie her on the horse again, but he did. Then he stood for a long time gazing down their back trail before mounting up and leading her mare across a tranquil meadow.

Far into the morning Kling startled her by beginning to talk. At first she paid little attention to what he said, for her thoughts were with Reed, wherever he might be.

"...if I'd a known he was Race Brannigan's boy when we met in Wyoming...but I didn't...not till later when I went through his stuff and found that deerskin bag. Had Brannigan's mark on it, like ever other thing a his. Wonder he didn't mark my woman. Your man's mama, you know. Bright Fox."

She finally realized Kling was talking about Reed. "Bright Fox? Wasn't that Reed's mama's name? The Sioux woman?"

"Squaw, she was. What I said, wasn't it? So he did tell you. She was my woman first, though, before Race Brannigan and his charming ways come along." His chuckle was diabolical. "For a while I thought there might actually be a chance I was the boy's father, you understand? But later I figured out that she had been gone from me a tad too long. So Race and his whelp killed my Bright Fox. And dear God, she was a purdy little thing."

Tressie felt disoriented. Memories of Bitter Leaf and Caleb somehow got all tangled up with the tale Kling told. What was he saying? That Reed's mama had been wife to Dooley Kling? How could that be? And who was this Race Brannigan? Didn't Reed carry his own daddy's name?

The giant man rode in silence for so long Tressie decided he wasn't going to finish his story, but he finally took it up again, after their horses had worked their way slowly and carefully along the narrow lip of a canyon.

As they continued their slow crawl up the face of the mountain, she craned her neck to see behind and below. Surely if she looked hard enough she would see the lone rider that would be Reed Bannon. But the growth of pine and aspen and jagged outcropping of rock prevented seeing much of anything but deep and impassable gorges.

Kling's harsh voice brought her back. "Bitter Leaf did remind me a little of Bright Fox, but she was dumb as dirt, that girl. And Bright Fox, well, she fit her name to a tee. Bright and smart and quick. Didn't speak a word of English; still, I never had to say a thing twice to her, she caught on that quick. Tanned me a dozen buffalo hides our first year. Do you know what that's worth to a man like me? A trader?" Kling snorted. "Hell, 'course you don't, with your lily-white hands and puny body."

"If I'm so worthless, why don't you just let me go?" Tressie asked. A brutal hate eating at her insides made her sick. This was real hate, not what she felt for Papa. Then what was that emotion, and how could she deal with it?

"You ain't worthless," he said. "I need you for bait. I just wanted you to know what that woman meant to me, so you could see I'm within my rights to pay back the son for him and his father's sins."

Her mind skittered around, trying to follow. "Reed never even knew his father," she finally argued.

"Don't make any difference. He's still the son of Race Brannigan, and his birthing killed my woman."

"And that's why you're doing…this?" It was difficult to believe that a man could spend months, maybe years, for all she knew, getting back at a man for stealing his wife.

"Don't make light of this, you little slut," Kling shouted, and jerked on the mare's reins, causing her to toss her head and kick out backward.

Tressie slipped sideways. Frantically she hugged the mare's heaving sides with both knees and shuddered. On her right a sheer precipice plunged into rugged oblivion; on her left the mountain pierced the sky. At any moment she and the mare could plunge to their deaths. She bit her lip bloody to keep from crying out and giving this monster satisfaction.

Why didn't Reed come? He surely couldn't be far behind. This madman was liable to kill her, maybe even himself, if something didn't happen soon.

In early afternoon, with the hot sun beating down mercilessly, the two riders reached an escarpment about twenty feet wide. Underfoot the sienna bedrock flared around the face of the mountain for about two dozen yards. Scrubby brush and grasses grew through narrow cracks in the smooth stone. Otherwise it was as clean as if it had been swept.

Tressie breathed a tremendous sigh of relief when Kling

dismounted and freed her to do the same. The climb had been exhausting for both riders and animals. Perhaps he would camp here for the night.

To her great relief he did not retie her ankles and wrists, but went to stand on the rimrock, gazing down the way they had come. Maybe he would fall and break his dirty neck. Tressie rubbed miserably at her numb legs. After riding tightly bound for so long, she couldn't stand, and so remained sprawled where he'd dragged her off the horse.

She again eyed the mammoth back of her captor. One hefty push and he'd go over, tumbling end over end, maybe for miles before what was left of his scroungy body bounced to a stop. She crabbed awkwardly toward him, crawling, scooting, moving on hands and bare feet. When she was near enough to smell him, she paused for an instant to slow down her rapid breathing, the pattering of her heart he was sure to hear. Around them fell a great stillness broken only by the *Screee* of a hawk high above and the whistle of wind.

Just as she raised from the half crouch, both hands reaching for a spot between his shoulder blades, Kling roared and half turned. "He's down there, I saw the—"

At that precise instant he caught sight of her, ready to shove him over the edge, and backhanded her. She tumbled some ten or fifteen feet.

Knocked half silly, she shook her head and tried to rise...to run. He was upon her too quickly. Dragging her up with one hairy paw, he belted her across the mouth and tossed her away like a huge cat playing with a mouse.

She bounced and rolled, vision cut by sharp bright flashes of light followed by total darkness. She sank into the abyss, sure she was dying.

When she came to, rawhide strips cut her ankles and wrists, tied so tightly the knots were gummy with her blood.

More blood ran over her forehead and into one eye. She hurt all over as if her body were one huge wound. And all she could think of, past the racking pain and fear, was that she was still alive and Kling had seen Reed coming. No matter what kind of effort it took, she couldn't let the brutal Dooley Kling kill the man she loved.

Reed came upon the leavings of Kling and Tressie's brief stay on the escarpment just at dark. And there he would spend the night. All along it had been impossible to travel at night because the fingernail of a moon set not long after sundown. On the desert one could travel by starshine, but not up here in the mountains. He tried not to think of traveling by starshine; that brought back too many memories of nights on the prairie with Tressie.

He didn't find the blood until the next morning.

Touching fingertips to the dried smear across the smooth rock, he felt for a moment her pain, the fear that must be riding with her. A deep hatred sickened him, assaulted his senses. He spread his palm over the place where she had lain, closed his eyes, and groaned.

"Tressie, darlin'. I'm coming," he whispered. "Be safe, I'm coming." The bright white realization that this time he wouldn't run away filled him with a sharp-edged purpose.

There was only one way off the escarpment besides the way he had come: a tenuous, almost invisible path skirting the back side of the mountain. He took it, riding slowly and carefully.

Kling had made sure there would be no mistaking the route he had taken, for a strip of cloth from Tressie's faded flannel shirt hung like a flag on a dried shrub clinging to the lower edge of the trail. The scrap of fabric had a smear of blood on it, as if the son of a bitch were mocking him, saying, if he had so chosen she could be at the bottom of this ravine littered with tumbled boulders the size of houses.

At midday Reed rode up on two horses, one of them Tressie's, calmly grazing in a patch of scrubby grass. And far above he spotted two figures moving like tiny ants along a narrow ledge, heading precariously toward the snowy cap of the great mountain. His heart nearly stopped. At least she was alive, but where in God's name was Kling taking her? And why?

If he had wanted to kill Reed, or for that matter the both of them, he could have done so easily. There was most surely only a mad reasoning behind this wild flight to the top of the world.

On impulse Reed cupped his hands around his mouth and shouted a war cry from his childhood. The shrill tones ululated across the wilderness chasms, bounced back and forth from cliffs to bluffs to mountaintops. Tressie's mare screamed, her head tilted upward and lips curled back as if she understood precisely what was going on.

Reed unsaddled his gelding, worked off the bridle, and rubbed at the velvety nose. "See ya later, pal."

For a moment he considered his options. He had a pocketful of jerky and he hooked the canteen over his head and under one arm. The mackinaw and bedroll he fastened on like a backpack. When he found her, she would be cold, so he had to take them. Last, he studied the rifle. It represented extra weight, and regretfully he left it behind, choosing instead the long-bladed knife, which he inserted in the backpack.

Tressie and Kling reached the cave when it was almost too dark to see anything.

For the last few hours, ever since hearing Reed's shrill yodel, she had moved as if in a trance. She thought of nothing, felt nothing. Just kept moving. She must stay alive, she had to. Not for hate, but for love.

Kling climbed behind her and when she faltered he'd shove her upward. At times she yearned to let go and take him with her. But there was Reed down below and on his way. She imagined him holding her safe in his arms, and continued to crawl across the windswept face of the mountain.

Above the shelf onto which Kling had shoved her, snow blanketed the rocks. No longer intent on climbing, she began to shiver from the cold.

Kling bumped her forward. "In there. Get inside."

Tressie stumbled on stone-bruised and battered feet, into the pitch-blackness of a cave. The cold hard floor sloped sharply downward and she fell, fetching up finally when the rock flattened out. The air was dank and remarkably warmer than outside. She kept very still, listening for Kling. Maybe the bastard would fall and break his neck.

But when he did come, he trod easily down the incline. He carried a small armload of wood he'd obviously gathered around the cave's entrance. It didn't take him long to build a small fire.

Seeking the welcome warmth and light, Tressie asked in a faint voice, "Where are we?"

"Where we belong," Kling replied. "A final resting place, of sorts. He'll be here come morning. And then it'll all be over but his suffering. And that will go on as long as he remembers how you died. And he'll remember, I'll see to that."

The fire's warmth washed over her and she felt herself drifting off to sleep. That frightened her and she shook her head, rubbing at both eyes. She was having trouble concentrating on the meaning of his words. Kill her and not Reed? She didn't comprehend.

"What are you going to do?"

"You struck color down yonder, you and him, didn't you?" The question was a snarl of contempt.

'You were watching. Surely you know."

"Don't get smart with me, girl. Yes or no will do."

She didn't answer, but moved even farther away from his threatening bulk. From there she could see his fearful face reflected in the glow of the flames.

He roared, "I said, yes or no."

She flinched and hugged herself, her teeth chattering madly. She didn't even remember what he had asked, but replied anyway. 'Yes." She supported herself with both arms, propping them behind her, and disturbed something that rolled on the stone floor, setting up a noisy clatter.

"What was that?" Kling shouted.

He was nervous, perhaps even a little scared of what was yet to come. Good, he very well should be. Reed was going to kill him if she didn't do the job first. Deep down in her bones, she knew that.

Looking around at the walls of the cavern, she said, "I don't know. It came from in there."

She pointed deeper into the cave and scooted back out of the firelight so that she disappeared from his view. Something cool and smooth lay against her leg and she explored it with the fingers of one hand. It was round with two deep-set cavities on one side...like eyes! She clutched the thing, came up with it. Dragged in a harsh breath. A human skull stared back at her and it took every ounce of courage she could muster to hang on to it.

"Dooley, is this sacred ground? Indian burial ground?"

He grunted, muttered, "Where you at, girl? There ain't no place you can go. Better git yourself back here where I can see you."

She sighed and inched forward into the firelight. "Is it true that the Indian spirits guard their sacred ground? I heard they can even kill anyone who strays where they don't belong."

"Bull. That's pure bull. No such thing as spirits."

"Would you like to sleep in a graveyard?" Tressie asked after a moment's pause.

"Well, 'course not, but that's different."

"Is it?" Tressie had been almost ready to show him the skull when a thought, occurred to her. The man was already on edge. If she could get him nervous and overwrought before Reed arrived, then maybe she could distract him with the skull at the proper time. Frightened, he might make a mistake that would give Reed the advantage. Kling was a huge man, strong and vicious, and Reed would be no match for him physically.

She cradled the fearful object in her lap and asked *sotto voce*, "Do you ever dream of Bright Fox or Bitter Leaf?"

"Dream? Woman, grown men don't dream. I'm gonna fix some coffee. Git yourself on over here by the fire where I can see you."

She didn't move, but persisted, "Surely you think about them. Where their spirits are. Their people place a lot of faith in the spirit world, I hear. Suppose Bitter Leaf knew what you did to Caleb. What do you think she would do?"

"Do?" Kling coughed out a laugh. "What could she do? Dumb little slut."

Tressie said very softly, "A mother's love is fierce. I wouldn't be surprised but what her spirit might skin you alive. I wouldn't want to fall asleep and wake up to find a fearsome Indian spirit skinning me like game."

"It ain't spirits that bother me, it's gals like you who go on and on. Besides, if I was to worry any about haints, it'd be that Bright Fox would fault me not stealing her back from that filth Race Brannigan."

"Why did you desert your son, leave him with strangers?"

"I said shut up! What'd you do with the boy, anyway? You ain't so high and mighty or you would have took care of him."

"Caleb...Caleb died. I tried to save him. I loved him like he was my own, but I couldn't stop him from dying." She choked down a sob.

Kling banged the coffeepot down near the fire. "Enough, woman. Enough. I don't want to hear no more about the little half-breed brat."

She felt a burning in her throat. She didn't want to start crying, for fear she would never stop. "He was your son. How can you be so callous?"

"He killed his mama."

"That wasn't his fault."

"Shut up, girl. What do you know? Of course it was his fault. Whose, then, if not his?"

She supposed men like this had to find someone else to blame for all their troubles, no matter what. "Is that why you want to hurt Reed? Because you think it was his fault that Bright Fox died?"

"His daddy took my life." The huge man actually sounded as if he were about to cry.

"But you had Bitter Leaf."

"Not the woman only—women only ain't worth this. He shouldn't a took everything that was mine. I had my wagon, my trade, folks looked up to me. Even the Indians would trade with Dooley Kling. Until Brannigan come along with his oily ways. Lying and cheating, selling them whiskey."

Tressie wondered briefly what had happened to Race, decided it didn't really matter. "But that's still no reason to—"

Kling launched himself at her, grabbing her shoulders and shaking, pounding her about the head.

She cried out and struggled with him.

He threw her backward, tired of the game. "I told you to shut up."

She curled up where she fell, eyes filling with tears.

This monster was beyond remorse. Out there somewhere was the man she would always love. Her need to seek revenge on Papa faded and was gone. She'd beheld the ugliness of such desire in the face of a beast. Never again would she long to see Papa's expression when he learned of Mama's death. At last she could let him go to meet his fate, whatever it might be. Her own destiny lay with the man coming for her.

Slowly and quietly she crawled along the cave floor until she found the skull. She fell asleep with it clutched in her arms.

Kling awoke her, hovering inches from her face, his own features pulled tight in anger.

Through hot tears of fright she tried to read the maniacal expression there. What she saw made her whimper. He had most surely gone mad, and she feared she, too, was headed in the same direction.

"I heard him," Kling hissed. "It must be daybreak. He's coming. Git up."

Kling kicked at her and Tressie tried to scramble to her feet, but the skull came up between them. The flickering firelight cast eerie shadows across the empty eye sockets and in the ghastly hole where a nose had once been. The mouth filled with teeth grinned, all the more terrifying because of the missing lower jaw.

Kling's eyes rolled wildly. "Bitch," he screamed, and fell back away from her. "I saw you walking. You did this to me!" He pointed a trembling finger at Tressie.

He had gone mad. She dropped the skull and scrabbled up the incline, heading for the cave opening.

Kling lunged, grabbed her by the back of her shirt, and flung her down into the unholy darkness below the fire.

She screamed and flailed along the smooth floor for a handhold. It seemed as if she fell forever.

Kling roared and stumbled after her. "No, I need you here for when he comes. He has to pay with your pain. Come back! Come *baaaaack*."

She tumbled up against something hard and unforgiving that bruised and battered her but stopped her descent. The harsh rasp of her own heavy breathing echoed from below. She rested in a curve of the cave's wall on the edge of a precipice. Rocks clattered around her and then dropped away into nothing. She never heard them hit bottom.

The darkness was so complete she could almost see more with her eyes closed. Quieting the harsh breathing, she listened for the sound of Dooley Kling coming after her, but heard nothing.

Was he going to leave her here? How would she get out? Even if he left, she would be afraid to turn loose and start up. And what about Reed? He would surely be here soon. Had Kling gone back up there to lay in wait for him?

Reed began to climb as soon as the sky was light enough to reveal the shape of the mountain. The snow above gleamed and shimmered like a beacon. He reached the entrance to the cave to hear Dooley Kling shouting accusations in the voice of a madman.

With extreme care he crept into the cave, closing his eyes to accustom them to the blackness as he went. A fire burned ahead somewhat below the entrance, and it looked like the flickering eye of some kind of strange animal.

Kling continued to rave from down there somewhere. A huge shadow, thrown from the fire's glow, danced across the wall and roof of the cavern, then disappeared.

Reed hugged the stone and moved cautiously past the fire, testing each step so he'd make no noise. Then he heard Tressie scream, a scream that grew fainter and fainter, like she was falling away from him.

He shouted her name, his heart thudding hard enough to break free from his rib cage.

From the darkness, Kling bellowed and Reed turned to face that sound, knife held at the ready just below his waist.

He shifted one foot and kicked something that rolled along the stone floor.

At that moment, Kling arose from the blackness like an apparition. Firelight painted his huge figure in red and black. The thing bobbling noisily across the smooth floor met up with him. He stumbled, clawed the air, scrabbled with both feet. The skull bounced upward and at the last moment he grabbed at it, catching it in both arms before he fell backward.

His eerie scream echoed for a long, long time, and when the echoes ceased there was only the sound of a woman sobbing.

"Tressie?" Reed called, almost afraid to speak above a whisper. What he had seen nearly drove him crazy with fear.

The sobs quieted. Then, "Reed? Reed, is that you?"

His breath caught in his throat. Dear God, she was alive. "Where are you?"

She could scarcely answer. She was caught up in the splendor of her imaginings. Reed was safe, she was safe. Together they could do anything, but mostly they could be together, always.

"Down here," she cried. "But be careful, it's steep."

"You wait right there," he shouted, and she wanted to laugh. Where would she go?

"I'm going to get a light from the fire so I can see you. I'll get you out, darlin', I'll get you out."

She snuggled back into her niche. "I know you will, Reed. I know you will," she whispered.

Eleven

Through Tressie's tightly squinted eyelids, light from the torch wavered dimly. Even knowing Reed was nearby, she couldn't muster the courage to open her eyes and take in the danger of her situation. All she could do was cling to the rough outcropping that had halted her tumble into the hell that had claimed Dooley Kling.

Dragging in a deep, cleansing breath, she smelled the wood smoke and the dank surroundings of the cave, tasted the crisp mountain air, and experienced a release of fear. Not so much from the danger Kling represented. It was more like her own bitter emotions and the intense need to avenge her mother's death had simply slipped away.

'Tressie? Darlin', you still okay?"

Reed heard a response that was no word, but only a quivery sound. Surely it had to come from her. In his veins Indian blood pounded furiously to a drumbeat all its own, for this cave was sacred and forbidden. The spirits hovered in protest at being disturbed. He had no intention of bothering them any longer than was absolutely necessary, and he chanted a few consoling Sioux words remembered from his childhood to quiet their ire. All he wanted was the woman he loved wrapped in his arms far from this haunted place.

Flame from the torch threw grotesque dancing shadows around her hunkered figure. The cave's ceiling sloped inward so that he had to bend lower and lower as he moved toward her. By the time he could make out her wide eyes and trembling lips, he squatted on his haunches.

Holding the torch to one side, he extended his hand, palm up. "Honey, take my hand."

"I c—c—can't turn loose."

"Oh, sure you can. Look in my eyes and just let go. Put your hand here, darlin', where it belongs. Easy as can be."

She sobbed thickly, then dragged in a heavy breath and slowly unfolded one arm toward him. "Reed? Oh, Reed."

"I know, I know." His fingers closed around hers and he shuffled backward, putting gentle pressure on her to follow.

The rasp of their breathing and the crackling of the torch filled the cavern as they inched their way carefully up the sloping rock floor to the small fire. Under his touch she trembled, and he dropped the burning pieces of wood to hug her close.

She locked both arms around him so tightly he grunted.

"It was Dooley, Dooley Kling. Why, Reed? Who's Race?"

"My pa. Let's not talk about it. We've got to get you warm." Reed shrugged from the bedroll and mackinaw strapped to his back and spent several minutes bundling her near the fire.

Though she allowed him to wrap her securely, she protested when he sat her down. "Oh, I don't want to stay here. No, we can't stay in here, Reed. We've got to get out of here. I can't—"

Touching lips to the opening he'd left in the wrappings so she could breathe, he gentled her. "Hush, shhh, darlin', everything's okay. You need to rest, get your strength. Going back down the mountain will be harder than coming up."

"Nu-huh, it won't," she declared. "I'll be with you going down. Oh, God, he was going to kill me. Torture me in front of you and kill me. He said you and your pa killed his wife."

Reed flinched, sank down beside her and hugged her padded shoulders awkwardly. "It's a long story I'll tell you sometime. Or at least what I know of it. But he wasn't going to do anything. He just said that to scare you. I would never have let him do something like that to you. Don't you know by now? You are my life, my only life."

Love flowed over her as if it were a living, breathing thing.

"Oh, I'm so stupid sometimes."

"Only sometimes?" He smiled, teasing.

"You know what I mean. So set on hating my father and paying him back that I couldn't see the gift you were offering. I could have lost it all. And you know something? I don't even really hate Papa. Or if I did, I don't anymore. All the way here, seeing the way hate had turned Dooley Kling into such a terrible human being, I truly realized what you meant when you said my desire for vengeance would eat me alive."

He patted at her clumsily. Her words filled him with a joy he almost couldn't comprehend. Despite her ordeal, he wanted to shout with pure relief that they were both alive and together.

Dear God, to feel her body pressed to his. He resisted a desire to strip her down and check out every inch to make sure that monster hadn't left his mark on her. But she was shaking so hard he was afraid to unwrap her. He had to get her down off this icy precipice in one piece. That wouldn't be easy, with her bare feet and scant clothing.

"Reed?" The voice was weak but he could already hear the old Tressie coming through.

"What, darlin'?"

"Do you think we could go now?"

If only they could. "Honey, there's not enough daylight left to see us down off this mountain. I'm afraid we're going to have to spend the night right here, snug and warm."

"And surrounded by ghosts."

She shoved the drape of the mackinaw back off her head and peered out at him. Leaping fingers of flame danced shadows high on the walls. The bronze of his cheekbones gleamed and when he turned his full gaze on her; little flickers of light were reflected in the dark eyes. How she loved him, and how close she had come to losing that love. The thought made her shudder. If she had to stay in this cave overnight, at least he was with her, and that was a far better choice than she had had a scant hour ago.

"Reed, I'm sorry I've been such a baby."

He took her face between his hands and kissed her lightly on the tip of her nose. "You were very brave. You stayed alive." He lowered his aim and their lips met. The explosive sweetness of being together tinged the gentle kiss with ecstasy. The bedroll and mackinaw ended in a pile around them.

He'd thought to only hold her, keep her secure, because of all she'd been through, but she pressed against him with a fierce longing whether for succor or from desire he couldn't tell, and so he turned loose all his pent-up emotions. There in that sacred cave with the spirits of his ancestors looking down on them. Tressie and Reed at last came together with hope for the future, with no reservations from the past.

The next morning, while he fashioned wrappings from the tail of the mackinaw for her battered feet he finally remembered the letter from Rose that he had carried so carefully. After he tied the last strip of fabric around the clumsy but effective shoes, he sat beside her and, with dread for her sorrow, tried to tell her about her father.

"Yesterday…last night, I couldn't think of anything but that you were alive, that I hadn't lost you. But now it's time…I mean I think we'd better talk about your papa."

"Papa?" she whispered. "What about him?"

All these months searching, she never once considered she might not want to know if the news was bad.

"He's…I mean, there was this man… Oh, just let me read you Rose's letter. It explains it better than I can."

She listened without comment through Rose's tale of Cray and how he'd showed up in Virginia City with the tintype of Tressie and her mama, and how Rose had pried the story out of the miner with the help of a few gold nuggets. But when he came to the part where Cray told Rose about Evan Majors dying in the cave-in, she began to cry.

The huge tears that had shimmered along the bottom of her lids spilled over and poured down both cheeks. At first she made no sound, just sat there with her fists balled in her lap, those torn strips of cloth wrapped around her extended feet, and cried silent grieving tears. But then she hiccuped and swallowed hard and stopped crying.

After a moment's silence, she asked, "What else does she say?"

Reed caressed her gleaming cheek with the back of his hand, then produced a bandana from one of his pockets and wiped her face. "Just to make sure and not forget her and come see her if we're ever in Virginia City."

She nodded. She was filled with a great sadness over her father's death. Yet that sorrow paled somewhat when she realized that he had died sometime back while she was still searching for him with a heart filled with hate.

"It's odd, feeling this way," she said. "It's like I can at last see the possibility of a life besides that old one. And at the same time I know I'll cry more tears. When we're safe and down off this mountain. I cried over so many things after Mama died because I was so sad over losing her."

"Oh, Reed, I'm so glad I forgave Papa. That makes it easier somehow. But the worst thing, the very worst is that I didn't get to tell him, I didn't get to say 'I love you' to him. I didn't get to say good-bye."

She choked a bit over the words, and Reed laid a hand on

her arm, just to let her know he was there. It was best to stay quiet, let her talk it all out, and so he said nothing.

After a sniffle or two, she went on, "He could have been dying while I tended Mama at birth, or while I was burying her and the poor babe. Isn't it strange how things can run beside each other like that, and us not even know it? How you were down South fighting at the same time 1 was trying to survive in that soddy, and how we came together anyway?"

"It's been hard, Tressie. But it's over."

He paused, gazed at her with awe. How strong she was, how determined. And she loved him. They were going to have a wonderful life together. If not for the sadness of the occasion, he would whoop with joy.

He gestured toward the cave's opening where the morning sun blazed. "It's time to be happy, darlin', we've done it, we've come through."

A reluctant little chuckle broke from her throat, as if she were practicing feeling good again. The sound echoed through the dark chambers, setting off the spirits, who tossed the joyful noise back and out into the world.

Together they stood at the mouth of the cave. She clutched at his hand and gazed into the distance, seeing the promises, seeing their life together. In the brilliant sunlight the precipice fell away into a lush green valley broken by gleaming trails of icy snowmelt.

After a silent moment, they started down.

Velda Brotherton writes from her home perched on the side of a mountain against the Ozark National Forest. Branded as *Sexy, Dark and Gritty*, her work embraces the lives of gutsy women and heroes who are strong enough to deserve them. After a stint writing for a New York publisher, she has settled comfortably in with small publishers to produce novels in several genres.

Facebook: Author Velda Brotherton
Twitter: @veldabrotherton
www.veldabrotherton.com